# THE DANCING MOUNTAINS

*by*

Simie Nkala

ISBN: 978-1-916696-77-8

*Dedicated to my best friends,*
*my husband and my daughter.*
*The wind beneath my wings.*
*The source that sustains me.*
*Here is to both of you.*
*Thulani Nkala and Lindiwe Nkala.*
*Love, Mom*

CONTENTS        PAGE

# Endorsements

**Dr Nomvuyo Mahlangu- PhD Health Science Research.**

An extremely powerful and yet atypical depiction of a King's selection and coronation processes in the ultimate ethnocentric context. Dancing Mountains takes the reader through an unexpected mystical, mysterious and yet thrilling journey, of the lives of a humble, ordinary tribe's people steeped in their ancient Kingdom values and lifestyle. A proud people well bent on preserving their cultural norms while serving as gatekeepers against invasions and foreign adulteration of their culture.

The read is cohesive, succinct, comprehensive, knowledgeable, simple, understandable, believable, and captivating. Definitely a great tale that will draw the reader in to the end. This is the second book by this competent writer and she gets better each time. This is the future.

**Mpangazitha Prosper Dlodlo**
**Award Winning Playwrights and Creative.**

A beautifully crafted story of the Umzingwane kingdom, encapsulating in miniature the characteristics of Africa lost and imagined. We learn from this envied community that if the spirit of Ubuntu is to triumph there must be a symbiotic relationship between the spiritual and the physical and that calamities are often an indication spiritual declension. In their desperation to keep their utopia unadulterated ordinary people are endowed with wisdom and skill by experience and the gods to do extraordinary things.

Written in a simple rhythmic style of repeat and enlarge this body of work is nothing short of a masterpiece. Forceful and all-consuming explosive and colourful in its nature yet celebrative in its mourn of what has been lost to through the savagery of imperialism purporting to be civilization. I join the mountains as they dance and shower you with blessings for this timely offering.

**Dr Philani Lithandane Ndlovu**
**LLD, LLM International Economic Law, LLB and Dip Ed.**

This book tells a unique African story about issues that are deeply understood among African people. Only those that have lived through the experiences of the mysterious and supernatural prevalent in the African mountainsides possess the unsearchable depths of knowledge and understanding of the realities that abound in their immediate surroundings.

This is a highly captivating story based on a theme comparable to early African Writers such as Chinua Achebe of the Things fall apart claim. Contrary to popular belief that women were excluded from leadership among African societies, the accounts on the influential roles played by MaDlomo, Gog' uMhlongo and other women in the daily matters of the Kingdom dispel the fallacies of women's exclusion from the societal mainstream. On that note I say, Congratulations.

**Siphiwe Moyo**
**BA Honours in Community and Youth Development**
**MA in Refugee Integration**

The Dancing Mountains is a powerful African story that keeps the reader captivated and takes you through a journey to the Sacred Mountains. Thandiwe is a great example of what it means to be guided by those who have gone before you.

This book uncovers a mysterious and amazing life of an ethnic tribe, including their values and way of life. While this book is about a certain tribe, it will propel you to look deep into your own journey of life and wonder about many things if you are not already wondering. I urge you to read this book and discover an amazing piece about us for us by one of us. It is vivid and alive. A second book by this competent author and it is indeed the future

# Acknowledgements

The participation of the following people in this work has in more ways than one propelled it to success and so I would like to say thank you to them.

My husband and co-author Thulani Nkala for not only believing in me but encouraging me to keep going. Your faith and hard work has indeed given birth to this book. Thank you.

Thank you to the following for the reviews and endorsements.

Dr Nomvuyo Mahlangu- PhD Health Science Research.

Dr Philani Lithandane Ndlovu

LLD, LLM International Economic Law, LLB and Dip Ed.

Mpangazitha Prosper Dlodlo

Award Winning Playwrights and Creative.

Siphiwe Moyo

BA Honors in Community and Youth Development

MA in Refugee Integration

A big thank you to Kings Makhalima/MNJ King Promotions for the beautiful artwork and design of the book cover, your work is amazing.

Thank you to PublishNation for their involvement in the publishing of the book, your work is much appreciated.

Thank you to family and friends for all the encouragement and positivity, the love, inspiration and faith which kept us all going in our various efforts to see this work through. Much appreciated.

...one of the two racers was going to be unlucky any minute now. Lightning struck as the bull had its horns around a tree. It struck only the tree, and it gave way. As the tree went apart and eventually down, it took the bull. Minutes after that the bull was no more. The strike was too intense. It couldn't have survived.
In the last glimmer of its eyes, there was a moment where it said judging by what had been happening to me since yesterday, I knew I would die anyway, but my last race was still a total package. And soon, that moment passed.

# MaDlomo
# The Kingdom Pillar

UMzingwane kingdom existed almost to its entirety on the shoulders of its women. The women were significant because they were warriors and the backbone of the kingdom. They led them into wars and won battles. Their advice and directive never fell on deaf ears. They were the cornerstones. They led them out of spiritual nets and guided them to safety. Major decisions were rarely taken without consulting them.

One of these key women was *MaDlomo* (daughter of Dlomo). She was a daughter-in-law to the Mhlongo family who was married to their firstborn son Hawulezwe Mhlongo. On her shoulders rested most of the responsibilities of this kingdom's daily running and life.

Through this woman, a son had been born to carry over from his father and the current king. The ancestry of this kingdom had chosen him before his birth. No one knew that because it had not yet been revealed to the people. The son was named Nsikayezwe. The legacy of the Mhlongos and the life of the uMzingwane kingdom would be perpetuated through him. Nsika had an older brother named Bhekizwe. The two were the sons with whom the couple was blessed.

UMaDlomo was known for perfection, speed and accuracy. She was known to pace up and anyone working with her at any point had to be alert. She was also known for her humour. She was a warm, loving and caring person. To many, she was a role model, a mother and a teacher.

Her birth name was Thandiwe Dlomo although growing up she was known as Thandi which was the first part of her name.

Short in stature, slim built with fair skin, she was now in her mid-forties. A force to reckon with. Though she was always strong to almost everyone she bore a lot of scars.

Life had not been so kind to her. Born to her parents at a rather old age, they viewed her as a miracle baby as they had no hope left that they would bear another child. So, when she was born, they named her Thandiwe which meant the loved one. She was a symbol of love for them as they believed their ancestors remembered them with love at an old age.

At the age of ten years tragedy struck and she was left an orphan. She was then left in the care of a distant aunt who neither cared for her nor was bothered about her well-being. Nonetheless, she grew.

Her chestnut eyes and beautiful smile always earned her attention from childhood. Her aunt wasn't particularly amused that the child was loved by people and was also a lovely child. She didn't care at all about anything which had to do with her. To her, she was a burden, but people carried each other's burdens in this community, so she had to carry them without voicing her disapproval of her position as a caregiver to this child.

From her childhood, she had rare qualities, and the village couldn't stop noticing or talking about her attributes and wisdom was one of those. This aunt of hers did not have children of her own and that meant she was going to double up on the girl and boy duties for this family.

When she finished her house chores, she would head out to herd cattle with the boys. It was a routine that in no time she got used to and learnt the skill of juggling between the two responsibilities.

This however put her in an abusive position as the boys found it amusing that a girl was herding cattle when their sisters were left at home. This made her to mature quickly. Sometimes she would talk herself out of challenges but when talking yielded no results she had to fight her way out.

Soon, she became a great fighter whom the boys became afraid of, and it earned her respect. Word spread fast and everyone began to know about the she-warrior in uMzingwane who was not afraid of anything or anyone. Herding cattle then became easier and fun for her as sometimes she would demand that the boys look after her herd while she rested and if any one of them got astray there was hell to pay so they did so with caution.

She became the queen of the wild. For every abuse she suffered at home she was compensated with free reign and peace in the forest. Thus, as every sun rose signalling a new day she couldn't wait to go out and herd the cattle.

At home, she earned a lot of beatings even without cause. Her aunt was a very mean woman. She also got used to that as there was no way out. At times she was denied proper food for days and survived only on wild fruits and the food she got from the fellow boys she herded cattle with.

One day she went out to herd cattle as usual, but luck was not with her. Unbeknown to her a calf went missing and that was a door to the misery she bore next. Whether the calf had truly gone missing, or her aunt's husband just played tricks with her was left a mystery as no one found out but the calf somehow mysteriously reappeared and no one accounted for how that happened.

She was very sure that the calf had remained behind when she left. As a norm, the calves did not always go with the herd to the fields but remained behind for security reasons. There were dangerous animals that could prey on the calves and there was the danger of easily getting mixed up with other herds and eventually lost. So, she was unsure whether the accusation that she had lost the calf was true.

Thandi was tired and hungry. They did not offer her any food but threatened that if she did not find it, she wasn't going to eat until she brought it home. She dreaded going into the fields after dark as there were scary stories told about the fields at night.

Some said people were seen with hunting spears in the fields. Some said if you passed the fields at night, you earned yourself a slap or soil will be poured on your head. Some said there were ghosts even, it was a long chain of different stories. Death was also spoken of even though there was no existing record of such. Scary myths and stories made people shun the fields at night.

She had to bring out her warrior self to be able to go back there. With every step, she took she felt like she was being followed. Every time she looked over her shoulder a shadow will be there and quickly fade. A heavy presence of a human being was felt within her, but she dismissed it as her crazy scared mind playing tricks on her.

She kept on going even though she did not know where she was going. If she had lost it, there was very little chance that she would make out the little calf from the bushes. Chances were also that it might have fallen asleep somewhere and was bound to walk around tomorrow.

She knew she couldn't go home without this calf, so she decided she would not go back at all. That night she was going to find a spot somewhere and sleep, then early morning she would continue her search and maybe find it then go home.

It was better to be scolded with the calf than without, so she set out to find a resting place. At least tomorrow there won't be repeated scolding moments as she would get there report the calf and resume duties of the day and soon after disappear back into the fields. She would also sleep during the day while the boys looked after her herd. It was a done deal.

Tears flooded her big eyes. It was at times like these that she missed her parents and wondered why they chose to leave her both at once. Had one of them been alive she was going to be home and safe today. She just didn't understand that death and life were both a part of the journey of living and in due time death located you and sometimes prematurely depending on the circumstances that cause your death, and one had no choices to make at that moment except to die.

She would be safe from the notorious people who lurked in dangerous bushes to pounce on innocent people. Safe from the ghosts and other scary stories of the fields. Real or imagined because of them people shunned the fields and yet she was here. All alone and helpless.

Leaning against one of the big trees in the fields, whether for balance or protection she surveyed her surroundings. It was now pitch black and she couldn't make out anything at first glance. Well, she might as well sleep under this tree, she thought and sat down.

She had come here scared of snakes. At this time of the year, especially the cobras and black mambas were plenty. As it looked now, she was spot on as there was not one but two on the tree, she had sought shelter under. The fight or flight response was triggered quite late when the two monsters had somehow fallen off the tree and landed right in front of her such that they blocked her way, and she couldn't run from where she was.

Petrified, she froze right there. The monstrous beings began to move whether it was toward her or in the opposite direction her mind had already seen how they will just jump on her somehow. The visualisation in her mind was so vivid that she made mistakes in the process.

She moved when she could have remained calm and silent watching the play out, this would have given her chances of escape. She panicked and eventually stepped on one of the snakes and it bit her, in a moment she blacked out and so she never saw or knew what happened to the two creatures. Were they even two or she had just imagined so, she wondered when she woke up at home surrounded by a multitude of villagers who had come in and she was not aware when.

The two giants soon left the scene of their crime and left her lying there, she was not supposed to last long as they were venomous. Two guardian angels happened to be passing by at that very moment and picked her up after tying her foot and restricting the poison, only the infinite knew what else they did because somehow, she survived.

They then took her to the nearest homestead looking for help for the little girl who was found bitten by what looked like a snake in the nearby forest. This happened to be her aunt's home and that was how they recognised her and screamed their lungs out to attract the neighbours who came pouring in afterwards and quickly ran to fetch Madlenya the community traditional healer who had vast knowledge of medicines for different venomous snake bites.

Madlenya had grown under the tutelage of her granny who was the healer of her time. In addition to her special gift and knowledge about different medicines, she was a community midwife. A very warm and loving woman whose smile was contagious. That was how Thandi survived and how the issue made its waves to the chief. A case of neglect was opened against the family and the chief gave both her aunt and uncle punishments that were due for their crime.

Midwifery was very important in this kingdom and midwives were respected a lot. These were guardians of life, as the portals of life opened to allow a new life into their communities' midwives made it a point that this happened successfully and safely. Madlenya was such a woman and had deep knowledge about safely separating the two lives.

She and other midwives also had great knowledge of the plants and natural medicines used to relieve the birthing mother of the pains of the process pre- and post-childbirth. This was a growing community and childbirth occurred frequently and such women were always on call and duty. Their knowledge and skill were much-needed services to both mother and child. She was always saving lives, in this form or that as evidenced by the moment she was called to save Thandiwe.

They tried to conceal the reason why Thandiwe was out at that time. The chief and people began to question the explanation given and it was found wanting. The truth soon came out. The neighbours had also heard her scolding and thought it had ended there so they gave witness which led to the two being found guilty of neglecting a child to the point of exposing her to life-threatening dangers.

One day while working the fields which was part of his punishment the uncle was bitten by the same type of snake that had bitten Thandiwe yet he didn't survive. The messengers that were guarding him to ensure he completed his duties every day soon reported to the chief and his body was buried in the community cemetery.

There was a lot of talk amongst the kingdom that the ancestors of the land were punishing him for the crimes against the little girl he and his wife had committed. His wife went into a state of depression after the passing on of her husband and therefore could not carry on with her punishment. The chief ruled that she should be let off and allowed to go and mourn her husband and maybe recover from the state she had fallen into.

Thandiwe moved into the village head's home. She grew up under their care and guidance. Her intelligence and resilience was admired by many. Her leadership skills later earned her some junior positions in the kingdom. Her new household encouraged and nurtured her skills and talents.

At the age of 21, she got married to Hawulesizwe Mhlongo. Hawu as the people in the kingdom called him was a son of a well-respected man. His family was also of great importance. Hawu's father was the rightful king of his time but never ruled.

Legend has it that a few months after his birth his father the reigning king passed on.

This led to the throne being passed on to a regent king who was an uncle to the then king. This was done with the hope that when Hawu's father grew up and was old enough to rule, he would be then given the reigns. Unfortunately, this never happened because that uncle also passed on when he was still too young and the reigns of power were passed onto another regent king whose son is the current king of uMzingwane.

Owing to all of this and because they knew the true history of things, Hawu's father and family were held in high esteem. It was also Hawu's father's decision to let things be as there were some in the kingdom who tried to stir the hornet's nest by encouraging him to claim back the kingship, as it was rightfully his. Blood was shed where issues of kingship were concerned, and he didn't want that happening as some tried to cling onto power.

He believed that the ancestors of the land knew everything and would equalise things when the time was right. Those were prophetic words as decades later his grandson was chosen to take the reigns and lead. It was also a different time and things were being done differently.

Hawu was older than Thandiwe, but they were a perfect match. His family had given up on encouraging him to find a life partner because he seemed uninterested until the time, he met Thandiwe. A spark was ignited and for the first time in his life he wanted to marry, and his father was overjoyed. He made sure that all the arrangements were done in no time. It was one very grand event and one that the people still spoke of and smiled about years after it had occurred.

Hawu admired Thandiwe's intellect among other things. She was beautiful and well- rounded, but her intellect came out tops. She challenged him and made him think on his feet and so he also became better. Better at leading, better at executing, delegating and etc.

One morning he had an interesting conversation with his wife. He was bemoaning the changes which have been brought to the kingdom by some of the people who joined them. Some of which were seemingly integrating with local customs and norms and looked as though they were a perfect fit.

"MaDlomo", he had called out to his wife. "Baba", she responded. "Do you realise that things are slowly changing in this kingdom?", he asked. "In what sense baba, she asked before continuing. Change can be a good thing, change can be a bad thing it largely depends on what has changed and why", she said.

There is so much talk about civilisation and development. Sometimes I feel like some of the people that have joined our kingdom do not fully appreciate our ways. What development and what civilisation are they talking about?, he asked as though to himself but he knew her wife's intelligent ear was listening. Addressing her directly he asked, what is civilisation and what is development MaDlomo?

"Do not trouble yourself baba about such matters. You see, people tend to confuse civilisation and development. Those are two different things.", she said. Mhlongo was now intently listening because from experience he knew when his wife went this deep into a matter it was just about to get solved.

"You see development is not a fine human skill or virtue, it is more about erecting physical structures and changing the physical layout of a place, or inventing new ways of doing things yet civilisation is a fine human skill which engages emotions and brains, it is the ability to put yourself in another's shoes, we call it uBuntu", said MaDlomo.

"So, are you implying that a person can be developed yet not civilised?", he asked. "Well, I am not saying anything, but you tell me this. If a person who has big weapons of an advanced nature attacks people with lesser or none of what he has, would you say he is civilised seeing his armoury will be well developed and advanced? Yes, his kind of armoury might be well developed and advanced but where is his civilisation?" She paused as he seemed to have slipped into deep thought.

"That is certainly a mouthful MaDlomo, not any and everyone can be quick to understand the differences. Now you understand why I am worried. She reminded him that this kingdom was under the blessing and guidance of the Source even if the changes he was bemoaning did have effects it will be a matter of time before the beginner and finisher of it all spoke and reacted to all those things especially if they were not in the best of the interests of the people.

On many levels, he agreed with her and believed they were faithful people. A cultured people. A breed whose being spoke volumes and should not be afraid of change. It was one such conversation he remembered every time things seemed to be unsettled in the kingdom, he knew the greater being was responsible for them and in good time would respond to any cause for alarm or cry for help.

This was the best couple to have come out of the uMzingwane kingdom. One that exchanged ideas, one that challenged each other, one that helped each other strive for better standards, one that was admired by many and blessed by the ancestors of the land.

# Welcome to the uMzingwane Kingdom

UMzingwane kingdom is an expanse of land whose heart curves around the mighty uMzingwane river, flowing and curving with it right into the sacred Dancing Mountains and Forest. Those in the know say that the name itself is telling as it is a portmanteau, a blend of two words, namely *umuzi* (home) and *Ngwane* (people who originated from Swaziland); therefore, it means 'Home of the Ngwanes'. The name itself is heavily contested as those who arrived here before the others felt it is not representative enough.

They argue that a name should not highlight one ethnic group over others as this gives a sense of entitlement and ownership over and above others. The uMzingwane kingdom was a conglomeration of different ethnic groups, consisting of those who arrived before the Ngwanes from Central Africa and other parts of Africa.

Like any progressive society, differences are encountered. However, what kept the people united was the expert nation-building skills of their leaders, their cultural values, and their spiritual grounding. They had several leaders in different areas who were led by their king, these included cultural and spiritual leaders. These leaders were the ones who King ensured that all the different ethnic groups blended in a way that made them dependent on each other. This perpetuated peace and respect among them.

The Ngwanes were natural warriors and had paved their way and existence through the spear and assimilation techniques. For this reason, they were responsible for the security of the kingdom and their military prowess came in handy. These were the *ibutho* (regiment) men that made the Godlwayo regiment whose history in battle was impeccable.

The cultural and spiritual matters of the kingdom were taken care of by the ethnic group amongst them called abeNyubi. AbeNyubi were known for their expert and intimate knowledge of the plants, their medicinal value, and their healing properties.

This knowledge and connection to the higher power whom they referred to as Source made them pillars in spiritual matters and so, for these reasons, they became the custodians of the kingdom's religious rites and customs. Most of them were the seers and spiritual advisers to the people, the chiefs and the king.

Its borders kissed the red soil plains of the Nkankezi Kingdom to the far east, hugging it to the Imilingo mountain ranges, and it meets the Mhlonyana kingdom at the foot of the Sesheli mountain range where the Somthoba river begins. These mountain ranges and rivers carry an exciting history with their names too.

History and folklore have it that they may have had different names before a time of war and differences amongst these kingdoms, a time which saw the renaming of these places according to occurrences that took place on or around them.

The Imilingo mountain range, for instance, is said to have gotten its name after a surprise attack that the Nkankezi kingdom unleashed on the uMzingwane Kingdom, and the ancestors blocked their attack, driving them all the way to the Imilingo mountain ranges, where a lot of bizarre happenings according to folklore occurred.

It is said that darkness engulfed the whole mountain expanse causing temporary blindness. They were eventually rescued but were never the same, which caused the two kingdoms to sign peace agreements and swear to work together for their kingdoms' greater peace and well-being.

The peace agreement worked well for the uMzingwane kingdom, but the same cannot be said about Nkankezi. The surprise attacks and all the problems they caused for the neighbouring kingdoms were born out of a sense of entitlement, one that ran for many years and the people felt this peace agreement interfered with their need to capture and take back what they called their ancestral land.

The Nkankezi folks had been staying here longer than any other kingdom. Upon arriving here decades back, they made it home, generations and generations of people dating back in their lineages had occupied this land, and to them, it was ancestral land.

Neighbouring kingdoms were born out of people who travelled this far and found this place charming enough to make a home. History has it that the Nkankezi folks did not like much anyone who came afterwads and preferred to be the only ones that lived in this area, thus why people who later arrived had to create their own kingdoms and not live directly with and or amongst the Nkankezi people.

Many people eventually trekked this far and made homes for themselves, which later caused the Nkankezi folks to feel like their land and space had been stolen, so from time to time they would be quarrels and fights over land and ownership.

When the peace agreement was eventually reached with uMzingwane, there were significant disagreements amongst the inhabitants of the Nkankezi kingdom. Some of the powerful leaders felt that it was a betrayal by their king, and others felt the king's decision was right.

Those who were not happy with the decision vowed to find their own ways to handle this matter in a way that would satisfy them. The rift became apparent in the times that followed that agreement, with other chiefs openly calling out the leadership on that decision. Some regiments also felt that they should have been left to fight for their ancestral land and control over it. If not to regain control, then maybe to conquer and have these people live under their rule.

The significant disagreements led to the main wing of Umkhonto regiment, who were on the king's side in this matter intervening and that was when the supposed order happened, but it was evident that an uprising could happen at any time as the rifts and differences grew every day. People disappeared as well, and no one could account for what was happening. The regiment which was very vocal about their dissatisfaction was fingered in most of those disappearances but there was no evidence to nail it on them.

Great fear engulfed the Nkankezi kingdom as random things happened, and it was evident somebody or some people wanted to overthrow the king and undo the peace agreements made with neighbouring kingdoms. Time would tell what was to happen in this kingdom. Plotters continued to plot while kingdom defenders continued to defend it and that was largely the thread on which the existence of this kingdom hung on.

The kingdom of uMzingwane on the other hand has always been known for being cultural and spiritual. From a distance, having heard all the stories that local folklore tells of them, one could be easily terrified but on a closer interaction with them, one encounters very warm people, loving, welcoming and very generous yet one still needs to tread carefully in and around the kingdom in case you temper with things or places that are sacred which could cause problems for them and yourself in the process.

The kingdom is also known for storms of different kinds. If the people, passers-by or anyone who came into the borders of this great kingdom failed to observe custom a warning storm might happen. That is why when visiting the uMzingwane kingdom one needed to keep close to local people who will then guide you on local customs.

The kingdom had three very important regions. These regions are very important for they house different pillars of this kingdom's food production, cattle rearing and cultural and spiritual places where they come together to either ask, give thanks or appease their ancestors in times of need.

Amabele region is known for its fertile black soils and its proximity to the uMzingwane river therefore housing the granaries of Mzingwane as harvests are good each year and thus where food is stored. There are fairly good rains across the whole kingdom, but some areas are far too close to the mountains and have little farming ground available.

Each rainy season the people come together to till the king's land so that there is enough food to store in the kingdom's granaries. People also had their pieces of land to farm in this region for their supplies. Even so, they helped one another to do so for they had no competition amongst themselves but believed when the next person has achieved something or has been helped then you too can relax in your achievements and enjoy in absolute peace.

This is where the culture of *ilima* (co-operation) and *ukusisa* (loaning) came in. Ilima culture epitomised that spirit of oneness as a people, people would come together to do different kinds of work/tasks. For example, a Mr Mathema needed to tend to his fields, the whole kingdom would come together with their draught animals and ploughs to till Mr Mathema's fields. This made the job easier and enjoyable, but above all, it promoted the spirit of ubuntu.

Ukusisa is another well-thought-out cultural practice which people need to reflect on deeply and see whether it could still be relevant today. What happened with ukusisa was very interesting. Firstly, there was a kingdom herd which belonged to the king and the people themselves would have contributed to the king's herd. The King would then ask his indunas to identify people within their communities who did not have cattle and the king would then loan them some cattle.

This is the first layer of the custom of ukusisa, the second was on a community level, within communities some people had large herds of cattle, and they would then loan them to locals who did not have any. The third layer of this custom was within families. Families would identify among themselves members in need and then loan them some cattle. The system ensured that no one suffered from the indignity of poverty.

What would then happen was that the cattle loaned to these individuals would multiply under their care, after a while the owner would ask for his cattle to be returned, but the cattle who were born during the loan tenure would remain with the person who was loaned the cattle. They did not just remain with him, but they effectively became his and he could loan them to others as well.

The culture equalised relationships and eliminated the indignity of poverty. There were no street kids or homeless people in the kingdom as each time a person fell into a spell of trouble the king and the leadership will intervene. There was a unity of purpose which saw them lending, assisting, and uplifting one another through the everyday challenges of life.

They also believed doing so was a service to the ancestors of the land and attracted blessings for oneself and ultimately for the whole kingdom. This belief kept them united and living peacefully. Punishment for wrongdoing was also very steep and none wanted to risk having to go through such.

Ezinkomeni region was where they did cattle rearing. Cattle were a very important part of the lives and belief systems of the people of uMzingwane. It was also regarded as a measure of wealth. There were several kingdom kraals across the Ezinkomeni region. This region had good feeding areas and had plenty of water seeing it was located where different kingdom rivers met and nearest to the mountain river which never ran dry.

Most of the families and people who lived in this region were experienced in cattle rearing and had large herds of cattle. Although people from other regions owned cattle, this region boasted of larger herds and most of which belonged to the kingdom.

There were people assigned the task of herding the kingdom's cattle and looking after their daily welfare. Every member of this great kingdom owned cattle, for those who didn't have any cattle the ukusisa culture would provide them with some and all went well.

No one was supposed to go hungry or lack while their neighbour or relatives had something. It was considered taboo and against the values of ubuntu which were the core values which bound and knit this whole kingdom together. They had a common saying which went like this-the noise from your neighbour's hungry children crying for bread will keep you awake at night and so for your peace of mind, you played your bit.

Differences were normal and solved amicably amongst the people or at the chief's indaba where he gave rulings. At best and at most, the aim was peaceful co-existence between the kingdom and the people of the kingdom.

Cattle were regarded as sacred animals in the kingdom. The ancestral spirit dwelled in a chosen bull. In most cases, the behaviour of this bull will change once picked and rituals performed to consecrate it to the ancestors. There was a story in the kingdom that once upon a time, the kingdom head had gone hunting and he did not return as expected.

The family bull which had been consecrated to the ancestors came to the homestead on its own and it would not leave even when people tried to chase it away, it only left when it was discovered that the headmen had died in the bush. No one knew the cause of his death and suspicion did round with others suspecting the lions in the area he was said to have gone hunting in.

Most people found it unbelievable that he had gone hunting alone which also raised more suspicion for he used to go with some of his men. When questioned his men said he asked them to remain behind and that he was not going to be long.

Some said he knew he was going to die on that day thus he wanted no one to witness his passing on. There was so much speculation, but the sad part was they had lost one of their own. It was finally widely believed that the ancestors of the land may have had a hand in it and possibly communicated with him to go alone to where he went.

Cattle were regarded as a measure of wealth and were dear to them. Marriage rites and ceremonies were not complete and recognised if the lobola ceremony had not been performed. In this lobola ceremony, there was an exchange of cattle between the families of the two people who intended to marry. This ritual was believed to seal a binding contract between these families and more especially the two who had chosen to marry.

A wristband was made from the skin of the slaughtered animal and its bile will be coiled and tied to it. This would be used as an artifact to establish a covenant between the living and the dead. This covenant was both physical and spiritual as this involved the exchange of ancestry and spiritual guardians that they believed watched over them.

When the exchange happened it meant that the woman was now a part of the family of her husband as a child who was to be watched over and guided by the ancestry of the family and the same acceptance applied to the man in the woman's family. In either family one then became either a son and or daughter and the agreement was binding for a lifetime as there was no divorce.

When you are married it was for a lifetime. If you encountered problems in that marriage both families were to be involved in helping you both find solutions to the problems and continue as husband and wife. At best they aimed at finding amicable solutions to life challenges, but no one was encouraged to leave her family or marital family based on problems.

The cattle also provided them with milk and beef in times of need and or pleasure. Any ceremony or celebration was not complete without slaughtering a cow or goat. Their bones were kept for spiritual purposes and the ones they didn't need were burnt. After slaughtering a cow its horns were used around the home, some would be put at the entrance of a home or by the door of a hut.

They were also used around the house as *inkezo* (gourd) that was used in rituals where communication with their ancestry became necessary. Most of their inkezo were made from dried calabash/bottle gourds. The animal skin was used in the making of amabhetshu (loin cloth) skirts for women and blankets they used to keep warm at night. They also used it to make *isigcabha* (mat) that women used to sit on.

The use of bottle gourds was very interesting. The gourds had varied uses around their homes. They were planted as a vegetable and used for food and medicine. When they dried up, they were used as containers, decorated as artifacts and ornaments. They were also used as instruments from which they made music and other healing sounds. They used them for rituals and as symbols in certain ceremonies. They were one of the important items found in and around the uMzingwane villages.

This region also boasted many goats. They also had special reverence and relationship with their goats who played equally the same role as their cows did. Where a cow was not slaughtered a goat would and the significance will be the same. Their ties and links to their ancestors through their animals were the same. It was a crime to mistreat animals.

The third and most important region was uMgogodla where the Dancing Mountains and Forest were located. The most frequently visited region as all the spiritual and cultural activities took place in this region. This is also the region where the King and higher leadership of the kingdom resided.

The spiritual leadership always needed to be close to where they had to conduct ceremonies whether with lightning speed where human life was involved or at a relaxed pace where their everyday normal activities were concerned, they still needed to be close to the sacred places.

That region was the backbone of the whole kingdom because disasters were averted there. Protection was requested there. Rains were requested for there. All the kingdom's important spiritual activities were held there. Thanksgiving ceremonies were also held in that region. The regions did break down into regions and villages but were well knit together and it was relatively easy to bring them together when the need arose.

The king was not always involved in everyday matters as he had chiefs and village heads who exercised oversight of everyday affairs. When village heads and chiefs failed to resolve a matter, it was then taken to the king.

When the king gave a ruling on such a matter it was then settled and not to be raised again. The king was also fair as he was held accountable to a council that oversaw the affairs of the kingdom and more importantly rulings that affected people's lives. He was also accountable to the ancestors of the land who appointed him to that position in the first place. These ancestors were believed to communicate directly with the king or via appointed seers of the kingdom.

If the king began to treat his subjects unfairly and rule according to the desires of his heart it was believed that the ancestors would forsake his kingship and calamity will strike the kingdom. According to folklore they had seen such occurrences before and would know the king was not heeding the advice of the council nor ruling fairly.

The Dancing Mountains was an evergreen expanse of land. Its vegetation never dried, and its rivers were ever flowing. A great part of this forest was made up of fruit-bearing trees whose fruits went across the seasons and throughout the year there was a natural supply of different kinds of fruits. Appointed people would go and culturally harvest these fruits, which will be distributed amongst the different regions at different times.

There was a ceremony called isipho semvelo loosely translated to nature's gift. The people would come together while the appointed people distribute the harvest of fruits after bringing it from the forest. People were allowed to take as much as they wanted to their homes. At other times kingdoms could receive fruit through messengers doing rounds in the regions.

This forest also housed the mystery of the mountain range called The Dancing Mountains. These mountains were believed to hum and dance literally from time to time and visitors or people from the kingdom could come in the company of the custodians of the kingdom's culture to watch this famous dance.

For some strange reason it always rained when this dance was held so you had to be prepared or the fun would be cut short for you when the downpours happened. Folklore also has it that if anyone did anything undesirable while they watched such dances, people could find themselves trapped in the mountains and now need some kind of rescue to be able to safely leave.

It was both a wonderful and yet scary place to go to. Anything could happen anytime and yet this was part of the beauty and uniqueness of this kingdom. People came visiting from far and wide to witness such and some even requested to stay as part of the kingdom after being charmed by the beauty and love of this kingdom. Those who were accepted to stay had to quickly learn the culture, language and practices of the people among many things, some of which took a sizeable amount of time to learn and perfect.

# Search for Answers

The dark ominous clouds were still lingering in the above sky. The wrath of the storm that had barely passed could still be felt. A bird or two were seen soaring into the sky but no one was sure if the storm was fully over yet. These storms were usual and frequent in this kingdom if the sacred Dancing Mountains were angry. The kingdom's elders would meet to consult Bab' uMhlongo on the cause of the storm and ask for forgiveness and so in the process, he would appease the mountains, then peace and calm returned to the kingdom.

Mlamuli Mhlongo who was known as Bab'uMhlongo in the kingdom was a seer. He had served his people from his late teens to his old age. He was trusted and was always accurate when it came to matters of the spirit. He alongside other trusted seers were consulted each time need arose. On their shoulders lied the responsibility of decoding spiritual communication and leading people in the way they should go. There were other seers across the kingdom who helped people with everyday life matters at a personal or family level.

When the storm had calmed down, the kingdom elders quickly made way to Bab' uMhlongo for enquiries on what was to be done if anything. On arrival they announced their presence as per custom and began to consult with him. "Did anyone go into the forest without my permission", hissed Bab' uMhlongo in what felt more like a curse than enquiry. "No father, not anyone that we know of, but we are yet to send messengers into the regions to find out", said the kingdom spokesperson who was known as Gumede.

Bab' uMhlongo made a consultation. There was a short silence followed by hissing and almost barking then long silence followed by the clearing of the throat. Two more minutes elapsed then Bab' uMhlongo rounded up a look at all the elders before he began to talk.

"Somebody is in the forest the mountains are not happy with the presence of that person. The release of that person will be dependent on how quick the spiritual appeasement procedure is done, ceremony performed, and that person identified", he said.

His voice battled calmness. In two days, a ceremony is to be performed. If not, that person will die. Their death will be upon you the kingdom elders because you are supposed to monitor the movement of people in and around this kingdom. He gave them a few more instructions and released them.

They asked no more questions. His last sentence had finality in it, the kind that tells you that's it, in more ways than one. It was upon several people, kingdom pillars and experts in the matters of spirituality to figure out how, where and when to perform this ceremony yet it was with speed that they were to do so.

Some ceremonies were held within the villages whilst some required that they go and camp by the sacred mountains until the ceremony was complete, which was decided upon by several spiritual leaders depending on what was wrong, and the process involved in trying to address that.

They desperately needed to know who was in the forest and what the motive was. Their second question was what exactly did they do to anger the mountains? As soon as they left Bab' uMhlongo's homestead they went to report to the chief. Decisions would be made after they had met with the chief to discuss this matter.

Mr Gumede led the way, he was trusted across the kingdom for his wisdom and ability to solve puzzles on the go. He was witty and very smart. A tall and handsome gentleman, who almost always wore *ibhetshu (loin cloth)* wherever he went. His traditional outfit summed up his personality and connectedness to the ancestry of the land.

He had two other men in his company with whom he was always found. They were as important as he was, he had become their spokesperson owing to his eloquence, soundness of mind and ability to express himself better than the others.

This trio worked so well together that you'd swear they were co-joined in a way. As their feet meet the ground, they made a sound as though a herd was moving. The urgency in their speed was apparent. They didn't have the luxury of time and were just lucky that all the people they needed at times like these lived a walking distance from each other.

Soon they arrived at the chief's homestead, and he was anticipating their arrival. "Sikhulekile silo sakithi' ngangendlovu wena obhekana lesitha enhlamvini zamehlo ugadle, Njomane ka Mgabhe, Bhebhe, Mhlongo, Makhedama", they all chorused the chief's praises as they awaited the directive to enter the premises of the chief.

This was their way of announcing their presence, especially in important spaces. This was their way of showing respect for their elders and the king's leadership, yet it was also their way of announcing their presence anywhere. If you visited a man's homestead you showed respect and requested entry by praising him and his people and asking for your peaceful entry. It was part of their traditions.

A messenger emerged from within the courtyard and told them that their presence was welcome, and that the chief was expecting them in his royal palace. This royal palace was where most major decisions and rulings took place. These men were familiar with this place as they were always here for this or that and so they thanked the messenger and quickly disappeared to where the chief was.

"Gumede, we all have seen the storm, what is the matter", the chief enquired after all the formal greetings had been done. He shook his head and sighed before responding. "Makhedama, *thole lesilo, (the lion's cub)* at this point we have no concrete knowledge of what may have happened or is happening. We have just come back from 'Bab' Mhlongo who also wanted answers we do not currently have". he paused and cleared his throat before continuing.

"Bab' Mhlongo made a consultation that seems to suggest that one of our own is out there and we immediately proceeded here from there", he said in closing. The chief stood up and started to pace, to a degree he was frustrated that there were still people amongst them that dared go to the mountains, yet everyone was aware of the consequences. He sat back down.

"I hear you Gumede, I do realise unfortunately that no matter how much we try to always regulate and monitor the movements of the people around our kingdom, one way or the other we will find ourselves in such a predicament. Did Bab'Mhlongo indicate any timeframes", he asked. "Yes, he said we have two days", responded Gumede.

"Well, that is our cue then, we must move fast. The first thing will be to check on the people in all the regions and see if we can find out who is missing", he said. They had a lengthy discussion on how they were going to do this after which the chief's messengers were called in.

"We all have seen the storm and I believe you seeing these men here know what it means", the chief said to his messengers. The messengers nodded in agreement and he continued. I will need you then to go into the regions and spread the word that the village heads are to check on their people and report back to Gumede and his men here. Each kingdom is to send their messengers with that report today before mid-day so that we know what needs to be done", he said in closing.

The messengers did not ask any questions, they rarely did if the message was straightforward. They just nodded their heads in agreement. After a few more instructions they disappeared into the regions to spread that message and the urgency behind it.

The people had already seen the storm and were awaiting instruction as to how to proceed. These were a very reliable lot, so everyone was guaranteed to get the message. In the elders' minds, the person who could have gone to the mountains was expected to be an older member of the kingdom.

Upon receiving the message, the village heads sent their messengers into the villages checking for people and asking if anyone was missing. Everyone was accounted for. None was missing.

The reports were then sent back to the elders at the Umgogodla region where decisions would be made as to what happens next. They did not ask about the children of the villages and did not include the children when they accounted for their people, a mistake they all in the three regions did.

The uMgogodla region had childminders seeing that it housed people who were almost always in motion doing this or that for their kingdom. When duty called, these women and families left their children with the childminders. They too did not report on whether the children were all present. Lessons were to be derived from any mistakes committed. Their children were as part of their kingdom as much as they were, and they needed to take note of that.

Upon receiving the reports from different parts of the uMzingwane kingdom, the elders concluded that the person in the forest must be a total stranger; one that did not know the custom of the kingdom. They arranged to go back to Bab' uMhlongo and report to him.

The mountains were feared and respected. Strangers however got caught up mostly picking fruits or watching the mountains dance if they happened to pass on a lucky day when the mountains were dancing. The dances were random and not easy to predict.

On arrival at Bab' uMhlongo's place, the elders reported all the people were accounted for. However, they could not confirm the whereabouts of all the children. They were convinced whoever was in the forest had no relations with their kingdom and or this village they are in and probably did not know their customs.

Bab' uMhlongo consulted the bones which told him one of their own was in the forest and a ceremony was to be performed quickly. They were confused, they failed to wrap their heads around this revelation. It was a confirmation, one they believed in and depended on through time immemorial, yet they still couldn't understand how it could have come to this moment. How their own ended up in the forest knowing how steep the price for that act will be.

The traditional ceremony was usually performed with the instruction of the chosen kingdom representative who was now an old grandmother in the Mhlongo clan who resided a stone's throw from Bab' uMhlongo's home. Gogo and Bab' Mhlongo's location in this region and kingdom played a key role because in times of need they were easily accessible.

They played a very important role in the well-being and day-to-day running of the affairs of this kingdom and so the people had great respect for them in this community. If they do not say a word or give an order for certain things to take place, then there would be no motion. Gogo Mhlongo and MaDlomo were female seers whose word and counsel steered the kingdom's ships.

In times like these, it is even of much importance for them to consult these two as it is a matter of life and death. The person's life depends on what they do now and how they do it, more so with what speed. So, they set off to persuade Gog' uMhlongo to instruct for the ceremony to be held before whoever is in the forest dies, especially since it was to be on their heads. None of them wanted to bear the death of someone on their conscience.

The spiritual connectedness and intelligence they had coupled with spiritual giftings allowed them to see into the future. To command and direct things. Most importantly it gave them that rare ability to travel between moments and worlds and come up with needed answers in and through any sticky situation.

She was ready for them. She was ready to help but needed to know who could have been so disrespectful. By this moment she expected and knew that they had run around looking for answers as to what happened and who did what but this time, they were so close yet so far from the happenings in the forest. They moved past the answer to their problems of the day with lightning speed in anticipation of a different answer but in the end, they were going to be led right back home. Right back to themselves and their omissions.

Even though they were equally baffled as to who had done such a thing, she gave instructions for the traditional ceremony to go ahead because she knew it was the only way to save a life. Whoever was in the forest would answer all their questions after being released.

So, they let it be. It was an uphill task. One they always had to do from time to time but never got used to. Every time they had to do it; it was like it was the very first time. The pressure mounted and the worry was always that if they made any mistakes lives were at stake.

This meant that they had to get on the move. Assuming the different positions that they usually take during the time of ceremonies they went. At this moment the ones that were going to be the busiest were the beer brewing crew. Though they always had a pot of beer reserved for emergencies like this one they were supposed to brew more.

Luckily though these people were not disorganised. They were so organised one would say it was not much trouble for them to go through a traditional ceremony. As they went on with their tasks one would say they were enjoying it.

They had learnt through time that being organised was their only key to efficiency. Also, they were not sure of the consequences if anyone was to be left under such circumstances trapped in the mountains. That person would most likely disappear for good though it was unknown whether their ancestors would have held them accountable.

One other factor which played a major role was respect for their culture and tradition. That respect went a long way in maintaining this level of organisation because disrespect towards each other was translated as disrespect for their culture and ancestors. The unity amongst these folks was of a higher grade.

After consulting with Gog' uMhlongo, the green light for the ceremony to begin was given. Soon after that, noises filled the air. Women grinding, young men cutting firewood, ululation as the work commenced. It was a great joy to watch and listen to. They just jelled with one another and carried on.

Laughter and shouting were the order of the moment. Some called for this while others called for that, so preparations would soon be complete. It was well. As the preparations continued, uMaDlomo was in a hut at the back of the Mhlongo homestead. She was consulting, looking out for the people and pleading with the ancestors on behalf of the people.

They did not reveal who was in the forest but promised that if all was done according to custom and all protocols observed, the person would be rescued. They warned that if anyone was to disrespect any part of this custom, the penalty was as known by everyone, death.

With an unclear signal, they indicated that some men were going to die due to disrespect and conduct which is not allowed in the kingdom. In her consultation, she could not see the faces of those men clearly, but from that moment she knew something bad would happen.

She left there and went straight to the chief to let him know. For some reason the chief's messenger could not let her in at that time but promised to notify the chief of her visit and then she quickly ran back to monitor the progress of things.

Deeply engrossed in the proceedings and everything, the messenger forgot to inform the chief of her visit and carried on with his duties. She couldn't go in without permission and invitation, so she continued with the tasks at hand.

Whenever that message flashed before her in a vision, she was greatly disturbed and burdened. However, the chief was unavailable for her to discuss this matter so she only pleaded with the ancestors of the land to guide the people and watch over them.

The water jars were quickly filled up and excess water was kept in the hut where ceremony stuff was kept. The boys swiftly returned from fetching firewood and those cutting and preparing it were done with the previous lot. A fire was made, and the beer brewing process began. It was time for the women to take over and they did.

These people were a blessed lot. Happy and full of life. Even under difficult circumstances, they did not fail to share humour and love. It made everything easier for them. Onlookers could be misled into thinking that this work was just a piece of cake when in practice it wasn't. Somehow, they loved doing it.

# Nsika in The Dancing Mountains

Crouched at the foot of a tree that grew from the foot of the mountain was twelve-year-old Nsikayezwe (Nsika) whose name meant the pillar of the nation. A prophetic name as he in real life was going to be the pillar to this nation. His hands were clasped together under one jaw. He looked cold and miserable with a pale face and innocent eyes with fear written all over him.

His hair and clothes were soaking wet. His bare toes dug deep into the mud. The chilly wind did not help his condition as it made him shiver. He longed for warmth. It had been raining and when it does rain in this kingdom or the sacred mountains it pours.

Nsika and the other children of the village were outside playing under the care of the childminders. Nsika and his brother Bhekisizwe were among those children. It was a fine cloudless day and people were in high spirits. The children were taking in most of the joy and loving it.

MaDlomo, Nsika's mother had long disappeared into her duties of the day. She had a lot on her shoulders almost every day, so it was convenient that there were people to look after the children in her absence. As they were playing a strange voice called out Nsika's name and he stopped playing for a while. His peers did not notice as they were too busy with play.

At that moment Nsika decided to find out who is calling him. This was not the first time this had happened. When he went out of sight the other kids believed it was part of the play, he was going to come back yet he would be gone for days and at that moment he too didn't know it.

The voice went on to say some things that sounded like chants or praises. Part of it sounded like his clan names but the voice grew faint as it disappeared into the direction of the forest. He could- not hear some of it and then decided to follow it and find out what this voice was on about, the greatest thing that pushed him was the need to prove himself to his family. He wanted to prove that his claims were not null but had substance to them.

Eager to prove to them that he was being called, he sneaked out of the kingdom and followed the voice in the direction it came from. In his young mind, his parents were going to be proud of him after he came back with proof that indeed he was being called. Little did he know that his call was larger than his little mind could comprehend. Larger than life itself.

On arrival at the forest being the kid he was, he began playing and picking fruit expecting that the person was going to call again, and this time give him a message to take home. According to custom even if he was being called by the ancestors, he was not to show up in the manner he did and alone in the forest, thus the mountains were enraged.

The fruits he had picked lay half covered by mud and water next to his small feet. He had not eaten much of it since soon after picking the fruits the storm began and he had been crouched under this tree since then.

He just wondered now that he felt lost and cold, why is it that his parents did not come looking for him? As cold as he was, he thought maybe they did not care, or they did not like the person who had called him thus why they are pretending it did not happen. 'Old people, he chuckled to himself.

On realising that he was lost and alone he had been a good boy, he did not scream or shout for help. People trapped by the mountains were not supposed to scream or make irritating noises. If they did the mountains would keep them longer than usual.

He saw a wet monkey jumping from one branch to the other and a thought crossed his mind. He needed to find the way home. He wanted to change into something dry and somehow get some warmth.

He had been crouched for far too long. His knees and feet were aching. It was even more painful with every step he took, after a few more steps his muscles relaxed, and he was able to walk freely although the irritating pain was still present with every step he trudged on.

In every direction he took, there was no way out. He walked in circles until he was too tired to keep walking. This was scary. He sat on a stone and tried to go down memory lane, from when he was playing just outside their homestead to when he heard that voice calling him to when the storm started.

It was all confusing. Not finding the way home and being out here in this forest alone was scary. However, for him being a chosen one the mountains were going to celebrate him and his presence with a hymn and dance.

Visitors could come into the forest in the company of Bab' Mhlongo to watch the famous dance. When they had been angered no one could come through just like today because of the raging storms and weather upsets. The storms could be intense, and it would not be much fun being out in such weather.

There was melodious humming from above his head and the mountains started dancing to it rhythmically. He stared in amazement, he just wondered who could have been humming and who did the clapping. Did the trees have hands to clap or was it just his mind playing tricks on him, he wondered.

It went on for a short while, after which the mountains settled. He spotted a cave in one of the mountains and moved quickly over to find cover. Had this cave opened earlier he would not have been this wet, he thought.

Inside the cave was a bit warm, he enjoyed his new place. His mind was still all over the place. That night, the storm raged on, but he now was under the warm arm of the mountain and felt safe.

After the famous dance, it began to rain again so everyone else in the mountain couldn't leave. Though it was unknown to him he had company in this forest. Since it was now heavily raining the cold was intensifying too. His companions were the victims of circumstance and carried the full wrath of this weather. The storm died down.

Howling winds followed the ceasefire. There was a breaking of tree branches in succession and then all went quiet. Calm returned eventually and thus when he fell asleep. He was not aware of his surroundings anymore.

A thought was on his mind before he fell asleep. Only if it didn't have so many consequences around being here this forest was a blessing. If only people could be allowed to just come here it would have been fun because he would bring his friends along too.

At his age he had seen and witnessed some things that most people only read or heard about, even some elders have never witnessed and so neither can confirm or deny. On this day was in a better position to confirm or deny such.

As he fell asleep, he resigned himself to waiting. Wait to live. Wait to die. Wait for an absolution that was maybe never going to come. By the time he woke up, he was still in a cave and feeling the presence of someone. Someone who had come in a dream and comforted him.

It was more real to him than a dream or a vision. The person was old and with grey hair, she wasn't alone. She came in the company of two others, a man, and a female and so that meant he was in the company of his great ancestors.

The voice was the same as the one that had been calling him all along. Sometimes at night but most times during the day when he was out playing with friends or just at home.

Several times, he had endeavoured to tell his parents that someone was calling him, but they discouraged him by dismissing his story without enquiring more about the issue. As seers of the land, they made a mistake. One that had consequences, this being the prince of the land they were all going to bear it.

He had seen them approaching at a distance and was instantly relieved that there were people he can depend on in this forest. As they neared, they called on him using his full name. They further went on to call on him in totems he didn't know but it felt very good. They neared.

When they arrived at the entrance of the cave, they asked him to rise and sit up. He obliged. The females ululated for a minute and then bowed. He thought they were bowing to the man in their midst. After which they came in. He was sitting.

Clearing the throat or attempting to do so, the male began to address him. "Nsikayezwe my grandson we are your great ancestors. You think you are lost but you are not. You came here today so that we meet and bless you for the journey that lies ahead of you which if you are not prepared will prove to be difficult.

You are the heir to the throne of leadership in the kingdom. The people will look up to you. All that you see happening before you is a reality of life, not a dream. You are not lost. You are home with the very people that will groom and nature you and yes guide you in the ways you should walk", he said and stopped.

Soon as he stopped talking the elderly woman in the middle began talking. She spoke in a shaky but finality-coated voice. He was intrigued though by the way she spoke. She wasn't quick to speak. She seemed to count her words before carefully uttering them.

She spoke in a fashion he had never heard but it was lovely and warm. It was intriguing and beautiful. Most of all it made him feel at home. The man was right when he said he was not lost but had come home because thus how he felt. Home.

When she finished speaking the third one began with her speech. This one was full of warning, firm but also full of love and adorable gestures. She also was telling him about the norms, culture and being of this great uMzingwane kingdom.

How they began. Where they came from, how they lived and behaved in the manner they did as a people and as a kingdom? She spoke about the responsibilities he was to carry from the first day of coronation to the last stage.

He didn't know anything about coronation or anything like it, but it felt like something beautiful. Something he began to feel warm thinking about, and he curiously looked forward to it. She spoke about the dangers in this leadership he was to take.

He had to understand all sides of this from childhood. He had to know that it was not only rosy and beautiful, dark days, and rainy days were also going to come and happen. He needed to be aware and ready for both the good and bad. And mostly be very articulate and brave in handling the bad ones.

He was in good company, and it felt good. The storm and getting lost became a distant story of yesterday. He didn't remember all those realities for a moment. He loved being here with these people. They were so fascinating, warm and loving. He felt so much love being with them.

Then the old man stood up and hovered above him. He felt his presence, it was consuming. As he stood above him, he spoke some words he didn't understand. He sounded like he was chanting something. Nsika didn't look up though he kept his head down and eyes fixed on the two women.

After a while, the man produced something which nearly looked like a pumpkin but with a handle to it otherwise known as *inkezo* in in their language. He sprinkled some liquid on him. After he was done, he held the boy's head a moment longer and blessed him. He then gave him a directive to move over to the two women. He did.

And stood a foot apart from them. He was told to kneel. As he did, they both simultaneously laid their right hands on either of his shoulders and blessed him. A blinding sharp light with a soft glow filled the cave. In a moment it was gone. It was back to darkness again.

Thus, when he woke up and jumped up to a sitting position but there was no one. He was completely alone. The voice was gone. The people were gone. There was no blinding light. It was just another day, and he was still in a cave and cold. The warmth and love were gone but he could still feel it and smell the presence of those people.

He went to look outside, nothing had changed. He was still in the sacred forest of the Dancing Mountains. Then it hit him it was a dream. The same people who had been calling him had visited him except he can't prove it to anyone. What a dream.

To him yes at this point it was a dream but, it was part of his coronation process. Today and here he had been coronated. Coronation was much deeper in the matters of culture and leadership of a whole kingdom. The people only knew the physical side that they were part of and whose ceremony was a joy to them, yet this matter had deeper roots.

The one chosen was coronated first by the ancestry in spiritual encounters and rituals they were not able to repeat to the people in simple terms. Those who went through it knew it was a delicate journey and process which could be easily subjected to scrutiny when revealed and so they kept the knowledge and applied its wisdom in matters of life.

He would live and walk in the presence of his great ancestors, even when troublesome times came, they would always be there with him to guide him and show him the way. They would also protect him when the need arose and punish his foes where necessary.

It was not always going to be rosy and sweet ahead, but rainy days were going to come, well stormy days in his case and he was going to need help dealing with those. This was the help for him.

Those who had served before him served under this same guidance. The love they have for the culture and their people was a result of this connection. It was an important part of their lives and an integral role player in the existence of such a people.

The quality of a leader had a lot to do with his connectedness to the roots of the people. Leaders who ascended the throne without the blessings of the ancestors and the Mighty One of this land failed dismally.

Their cunning craftiness was also the highway that led to their getting destroyed in the end. Their reign came to an end, either because of the calamities that would have befallen the land or those that would befall that individual and his lineage.

One such leader once took the reign of power, and his end was disastrous. It was one such fall that none could forget. It did not only affect him but his whole lineage paid the price of his cunningness.

Even after his death his bloodline continued to face difficulties, calamities, and unfortunate circumstances in succession. It went on for a good long while until the elders of the kingdom intervened and pleaded with the ancestors of the land.

After a while of pleading with the higher power and the spiritual leadership of the land, the families were relieved of the curse and burden. It was such circumstances which made the people tour the rightful lines either of cultural nominations or of everyday lives.

Like any other place, greedy people had lived in the kingdom before. Those who wrestled power from the chosen lineage of leadership, but it never lasted. It was also costly to the whole kingdom because in appeasing the ancestors when their wreath was unleashed every member of the kingdom participated.

It was a lot but as always, in the end, they managed to appease their ancestors and the higher power they believed in, and peace and order was restored. It was therefore a wonderful thing for them if at early stages before the subject of succession arose the ancestors provided them with an heir to the throne. This was going to be one such select occasion and time

# Ceremony Preparations

It is almost past midday the next day. The uMzingwane kingdom is a hive of activity. Women are grinding millet. The men are preparing to slaughter the bull for the ceremony. The boys have made a fire. The girls are out fetching water from the uMzingwane river.

All that is heard is different noises from different tasks and groups as they carry on. The day of the ceremony had been agreed upon which was to be a Wednesday. Thursday was also set aside for the welcoming ceremony when they come back with those rescued from the mountains.

In the centre of Gog,' Mhlongo's homestead was a big black mud pot with white spots. It was always full of home-brewed beer and kept sealed in cases of emergencies.

The sky was clearing up from the storm. This gave good hope to the people that the ceremonies were going to proceed and finish well. In anticipation of clear skies and no more storms after the ceremony, they cheerfully engaged in their duties.

Sometimes the skies didn't clear and that meant having to work under drizzle or rain and it was a difficult thing to do. The people of this kingdom observed their culture closely and did all in their power to retain order and peace. If it was disturbed in any way, it usually was taxing to restore it, so it was rather better to keep it good than to try and restore it later.

That being the case they had come a long way with this way of life. From generation to generation, they knew exactly what to do when the need arose. Tough as it was, they were a resilient lot too and were a proud nation.

The pride and love of who and what they were drove them. It carried them through the best and worst times, and they emerged better on the other side. In the end smiles of triumph and a promise of a better tomorrow is what they were left with.

Two messengers came in from Bab' Mhlongo to check on the proceedings and how the preparation for the ceremony was going. They checked every part of the proceedings not only because they were doing their duty but also because they too wanted this to be over so that peace and calm can return to their kingdom.

On completing their inspection, they bowed their heads in respect of the work being done, custom required them to do so, and appreciation also of the efforts of the people compelled them to do so. They left.

"How did you go", he asked upon their arrival. "Very well father and the work is nearing completion", responded the messengers in a choreographed manner. He nodded a long slow motioned nod and, in a voice, almost like a whisper said all is well is good enough. He gave them a few more instructions and released them.

In the backyard was a group of boys and girls practising some traditional songs and dances. Their spectacular dances were breath-taking. Even for those who had seen them perform before, they always seemed to be new each time they performed, and they always left the crowd hungry for more.

The night of the ceremony was accepted differently by all these people. For those too involved with the proceedings it was a long and hard night. They all wore regalia made from animal skin if it rained like tonight it proved to be a little too cold.

For the public, it was a night not to miss. The performances and songs were something to look forward to. The braais that accompanied the ceremony were not something to miss either.

It's now late afternoon and the people are ready to go, but first Bab' uMhlongo and Gog' uMhlongo were to go and ask for their peaceful entry into the forest. When entry was granted then he would dash back to the kingdom to collect everyone. Gog' uMhlongo will be left with her crew. She had a group of five people that she always went with into the forest or when she was to go outside her home for spiritual duties.

Mhlongo's arrival signalled for motion. Only the children aged twelve and below remained at home. Women who were childminders looked after them all night. When those going to the ceremony set off singing and drumming began.

Upon entering the sacred forest, Gogo welcomed them with ululation and chanting. "Welcome children of the soil, welcome children of the great uMzingwane ancestors.

Your ancestors are here with you, they are waiting to hear you speak, hear you sing, see you dance and be merry for happiness and prosperity is a portion they want for you and give to you always....", she would chant on until all the people are deep in the forest.

May peace and calm return to this great nation of people. May your great grandfathers and mothers grant you eternal peace and prosperity...she blessed them in the name of the Higher Power and pleaded with the Mighty One to look after the children of this kingdom.

Eternal peace never occurred for these people and their kingdom. All the times they had to come here eternal peace and calm were requested for and granted yet sooner or later something will go wrong, and the peace will once again be disturbed. Again, the mountains will be disturbed and angry, and a fresh need to appease them will arise.

The problem here is that even if the people toured the line and did everything by the book, passers-by and people who knew nothing about the customs of the kingdom on passing by were bound to upset the peace. At times the passers-by would pick fruits at a time deemed sacred by the locals or behave in ways that were unacceptable to the local customs, thus upsetting the peace of the land.

Today they were unknowingly gathered to rescue their king. The one who would carry further the legacy of the great uMzingwane kingdom. They were all doing themselves a favour. At this point did not know why they had been called to the forest.

"Operation rescue stranger", as they believed it be, was in full swing. Drumming could be heard at its maximum. Everything and everyone were now set on that course to rescue whoever was in the forest. Everyone was determined to see this over for all its worth.

The men with the bull had long gone ahead. They were supposed to slaughter it before everyone arrived. When everyone arrived, it was ceremony and braai time. The part everyone loved.

But this day there was a problem. The bull had broken free from the grip of its abductors and outran them. All this time they had been in the forest performing no ceremony rites but looking for the lost bull. Every moment that passed was heavier than the last for them.

The drummers and the women were nearing the forest but Gog' uMhlongo's usual ululation and chanting as the beast was being slaughtered was not heard. They thought maybe it was because of the drumming and quickly dismissed it for they used to hear it even with the drumming before.

Nevertheless, they decided to cross that bridge when they got to it. So they faithfully trudged on in their journey hoping all was well ahead. That hope was faint but even so, they did, not have any other option but to carry on.

On the other side of the forest, the search was intensifying with every second that passed. The bull ran twice as fast as the fastest man amongst them, eventually, it ran out of sight, and they were now searching for it as though they never had it to begin with.

The deadline also called for their attention adding to their frustration. They had just a day before whoever was trapped in the mountains disappeared for good. Today was to be used wisely to meet the deadline. Finding the bull and meeting the deadline were two unimaginable tasks for these men.

One man suggested they go back and report that this one had been lost and needed to be replaced. He was chewed to his very bones for suggesting such which in any sense was noble, but they were all afraid. Punishment was a bit severe in this kingdom it never was an option for any crime, so they rather looked for this one.

Drummers had now gone too far close to the mountains, but the silence was unusual. They stopped drumming to listen to possible activity, but none was detected. The silence was deafening and scary because it meant that something was wrong.

Bab' uMhlongo ordered them to stay where they were while he went to check proceedings. However, even to the drummers, it was clear that something was wrong. They just remained calm as they were about to find out. And soon.

# Nsika's Encounter
# with The Bull

From unfamiliar surroundings, Nsika woke up as one would do from a dream. He'd dreamt of waking up in a cave once but not like this. You dream and hope for things to happen for you, as it happens in today's movies, but you want it to feel different when it happens, you want it to feel more real, more visceral but that was not how he felt. He was plain scared.

He was still curled up in the cave his small mind wondering about as he was trying to inspect his surroundings. It was like being the main character in a horror movie, the difference being that it wasn't any fun. It hurt like it was expected to do in real life.

Slowly and carefully, he moved out of the cave. Finding a spot on a nearby rock he sat on it. He tried climbing down the memory lane once more, but the pieces didn't match up as vivid as he wanted them to.

The runaway bull had run itself into exhaustion. It was now spent but angry. The anger kept it moving. One such drama was awaiting this little fellow though because it had sought safety under a tree that was close to where he was.

As he stood up to move around, it caught sight of him. It was the first time it had seen movement and was keen to go over and try out its new opponent and see if this one would outrun it or if it was still the champion.

He heard a sound like the breaking of logs in succession. As he turned to see what it was, he saw the bull and instantly knew it was either the bull or him. The human sense of survival triggered the flight response and ordered him to do likewise. And he ran.

It was the fiercest race he had ever been involved in. Even for a million pounds, he would have never willingly contested in such. The difference here was that the ultimate prize was life. It was the survival of the fittest and he had to live so he ran.

Zigzagging through the forest they went. Whenever the bull thought it had caught up with him it was just another tree. This gave him more running time and space as the bull was yet to release its horns from the tree and continue.

The bull was enraged. Being tied down the day before and the heavy guiding as it was being led to a place known only to its abductors flared its temper. In this case, it was fun. Its freedom had been infringed the previous day and seeing another creature taking its previous position was great fun.

This fierce race angered the mountains. This kind of behaviour was not allowed here. Anyone or anything that passed here had to do so quietly, quickly, and silently even. This kind of behaviour could be welcome at the Olympics save only for the violence. It was all about culture and respect here.

One of the two racers was about to get unlucky any minute now. Lightning struck as the bull had its horns around a tree. It struck the tree down. As the tree went apart and eventually down, it took the bull along with it. Seconds after the bull was no more. The strike was too intense that it couldn't have survived.

In the last glimmer of its eyes, there was a moment when it said from what has been happening to me since yesterday, I knew I was going to die anyway but still my last race was the total package. And soon that moment passed.

The strike left poor Nsika in tatters. This movie was getting too real for him. In almost whisper he said now there is something you don't see every day. He was too scared to make any kind of sound or move but to get anywhere at all he had to lift those legs.

His legs had gone limp and a bit heavy to lift. He wondered as he looked at the bull that lay about a metre from him. Dead. He knew exactly who it could have been had it not been this bull. Him.

He sat down wondering how much more was he to encounter before actually getting home if he ever was to get home. He was hardened though, by this tough survival and was slowly accepting his circumstances and willing to survive even though.

As he stood up one thing was on his mind. He was suddenly tired of being the victim. If no one was going to rescue him, he then decided to be his own rescuer. Even as that had been decided he still stood there. Deciding.

It was so unbelievable that he had been away from home for so long, yet no one came looking for him, not his mother or father. If they did not worry that he was not home, then maybe they did not consider him important. These were the silent thoughts that kept creeping into his mind, and he would dismiss them. They were stronger each time they came back and more real than the last time.

He hadn't yet decided which one was true for his situation when he suddenly saw a frog jumping and playing in and out of the mud. He began wondering again from human beings to this frog and the universe at large.

The kid in him started playing and mission rescue myself was put on hold for some time. He stood there imagining the things he would be doing if he was this frog. The things he would do if he had such ability. A skill he began to envy as he watched the frog come and go within the water and ground.

He watched the frog come and go and wondered how is it that humans hide from the rain and shun the mud while this creature seemed to be having a wonderful time in this muddy water. It didn't seem to be worried that it was out in the mud or the open. He was impressed and enjoyed that moment.

Thoughts flooded his mind. That was the only thing that seemed to be doing rounds in his head. He couldn't stop them and yet wished he could. Even when he went quiet, he found himself thinking about the silence that had engulfed him at that moment. He was brave and scared simultaneously.

Sometimes doing things with a partner is quite an advantage. With a friend right now they would talk, decide together and at least carry the burden of being lost and directionless together. He was reminded that he was all by himself and had to carry on with the mission to rescue himself, so he began moving again.

He was half running and half walking. The problem was that he was running from the great unknown while running himself straight into the great unknown. He didn't have a clue about what was chasing him or what he was running himself into. And that was not good, but he kept moving still.

Not so-heavy downpours accompanied that bolt of lightning. Though he did not care he was slowly getting wet. He kept telling himself that he was born a survivor and will so make it out of this too. No matter what he had to face or how he faced it he was going to get home.

It was almost noon and Nsika was still walking. He had walked for many hours now but had no way home yet. There was a fact he kept shrugging, but it was becoming more and more apparent as he was trudging on the journey that he may never find a way home.

If he remembered well, it had not taken him two hours to get to this forest. Why then will it take him more to get back? This was becoming stressful. He felt conflicted as if many personalities were housed in one body. A scared young man, a brave young man, a decided young man and a confused one all at the same time.

When coming to the mountains, one uses a straight way ahead. When you are in the forest without permission, you are forced to walk far and wide. You are forced again to come back and start at the same old spot that you started at without your knowledge of the course. That was the power of the dancing mountains and forest.

Nsika had heard this story being told by the elders before. The women who looked after the children used to tell them these stories while the people were out doing ceremonies in the forest. Not that they ever fully believed but with age, they remembered the words of the elders.

In his case it was with the experience he remembered everything. He had never really believed or taken it seriously just like his age mates but today he was able to confirm and or lecture them better.

Had he kept moving towards the North he was going to meet up with the men that were supposedly going home. Now that he had turned around, he was headed to the dead man, the ones that decided on eating the fruits amid a crisis.

As he was approaching, he saw broken trees and fruits scattered all over. "Are there animals in this forest? If there are, are they dangerous?" he asked out loud. Maybe he was going to be eaten by dangerous wild animals was his final thought.

As he trudged on his way, he wasn't himself anymore. He was just a helpless reed that swayed every time the hope pipe puffed. He remembered his ordeal with the bull and thought maybe the bull was responsible for all these broken trees.

He decided to take a rest under one of the trees. His mind was now confusion controlled. In a minute he had it all figured out. He knew exactly the next step he would take and then have a sudden change of mind. Instead of doing what he initially set out to do, he would do the other, completely different.

There was a mahogany tree to his left at whose foot lay a soft granite rock he could lay on, relax a bit and maybe be able to refresh his memory. He wanted to go back to the drawing board hoping to be able to pick up the pieces of the puzzle and paste them from there.

It was a done deal. He lay on it and tried to reflect on everything that happened so far starting from home up to now. He lay just a few centimetres from one of the dead men. Unknown to him he had always had company from the moment he stepped into this forest except right now he was in the company of the dead.

This was however better company because the dead man wouldn't get to ask him questions as to how did he get there, what is he doing here doesn't he know he is not allowed to come to the sacred mountains? These kinds of questions were not so welcome to him now. They were only going to add to his confusion.

When he rested here it was supposed to be a brief rest then he continued his journey but unfortunately, he found himself napping already. He fell asleep for over an hour and so again he wasn't aware of his surroundings.

Soon as he blacked out, he had a dream. He dreamt that he was home with his brother and other children whom they played with. As they played there was a group of adults nearby going about their business. He decided to go over to where they were.

They were sitting around an open fire and roasting some meat. He could smell its sweet aroma as he came close. He loved spending time around elders, and they did not mind him; so, whenever he had a chance, he would.

As he got near, the elders seemed to disperse each in his direction. He was then attracted to one elder. On many occasions, this man had appeared in his dreams, and he had become familiar with his presence and voice.

He seemed to be uninterested in him today which was strange because he was always the one to approach him before and today, he was making effort. He decided to follow him to see where he was going.

While he was following him, the man disappeared before him. Nsika was very convinced that he had seen him, so he thought maybe he was slow, and the man was quick on his feet. He increased his pace. He began to run as he tried to catch up with him.

He couldn't find the man or see any trace of him, so he decided to turn back and go home. As he turned to go, he couldn't find his way and there seemed to have developed a river behind him. He was shocked and then decided to keep ahead. Turning again there is the river flooding and surrounding him.

As he stood there perplexed as to what just happened and how the old man reappeared and told him to follow him. He was relieved that there was help out of this.

The man went straight into the water and Nsika followed closely behind him. There was total silence as they crossed to the other end. That was a close shave, he thought as they walked ahead and eventually out of the water-bound zone.

As soon as they crossed the river the old man disappeared again, but this time Nsika was not bothered because he was confident the man would come back again especially when he needed him, so he felt safe.

This was great fun, so he had the protection and or guidance of some invisible being. Someone who came and went at will and in lightning speed. He wondered what other challenge could happen to warrant the help of that man.

A voice from above his head said, "Well done Nsikayezwe now you have completed your challenges and are ready for the crowning. Listening and following instructions takes great skill. Continue to master that art. You must remember no challenges are bigger than you. You are no ordinary person. Above the people, you will rule and above the animals you shall be king.

Everything and everyone shall bow down to you because you are the crown prince. The chosen king to the generation of my people. Be brave and never lose courage for at all times and through all things I shall be there to guide and help you", the voice said.

He looked up but could not see anything or anyone. He was used to this voice now and knew it was that old man who had said these things. At least he was proud of him even though he didn't rescue him this time.

He woke up from the dream. A dream that no matter how much you try to put its pieces together you just can't. The first part and the last part in unmatching pieces follow the middle part and so it puzzles you.

He stretched his legs and moved to a sitting position. As he was inspecting his new surroundings trying to read something into them, he saw it. Laying a few centimetres from him was a dead body.

He blinked in disbelief. When and how did this happen? Was it before he got here or after? Did it happen while he was asleep? How? One question after the other flooded his already confused mind. Questions he wasn't sure he would get answers to.

This might mean he is in the company of unknowns, he blinked at the thought. If this one is dead, then where are the living ones? How and why did they kill this one and leave him here for him to see yet not harm or scare him in any way? Once again that storm of questions poured heavily, and his small brain failed to keep up.

To get answers to all these questions he had to wait. Wait for the great unknown to shed light on itself to be understood. He was so scared he didn't even move closer to the body. He just hovered there like a lost spirit, looking up to the sky hoping for some divine intervention and or interpretation of all of this.

Another body was awaiting him. He was caught in his tracks by the sight of it. He stood frozen in his steps and looked around.

He was either inspecting for any other body or movement, something that might give him a clue as to what exactly was happening there.

There was no movement. It was quiet. He saw nothing but calm. So, he thought maybe they fought and killed each other. If that was the case, it was still a puzzle that their bodies were so far apart or the other one was trying to flee the crime scene and then just didn't make it. He concluded.

Now what, he queried? Do I continue this way, or do I change? He decided to change direction and as he did he walked straight onto another body. This time he concluded that it was the same body following him around. He was part of a huge drama again.

He closed his eyes and opened them again. He was trying to ensure that his mind was not playing tricks on him. It wasn't because the body was still there. This time he was afraid, and this was not good at all.

Fear was slowly gripping him, and he remembered the voice of the old man in the dream. Everything and everyone were to bow down to him and not him. He was not to be afraid because he was not an ordinary being.

That gave him a boost and he was able to remain calm. He decided then to closely inspect the situation he had found himself in and maybe find the meaning of all this. He moved closer to the body.

As he looked at this body, he noticed something that he had missed afore. These bodies were dressed in different clothing. This means that then they might have been together and only God knew what befell them.

If they had been fighting, then they couldn't have all died. There must be a survivor. Even if badly hurt and unable to walk, there must be a survivor or storyteller unless if he was the storyteller.

If it meant that he has company, then he had to find out in whose company he was. He could be in the company of dangerous animals who could devour him. He could be in the company of people, people who might have killed these people and could kill him also. He could also be in the unknown company of people who could assist him with his situation. As those thoughts crisscrossed his mind he bravely disappeared back into the forest.

Once again, the pipe of hope was puffing hard and he as a reed was bending in that direction. He set off this time hurrying with the hope of meeting somebody, dangerous or not... he was ready.

For a child, as he was it was not a case of boldness even though it played a role. It was a case of confusion. A need to get out. A wish for starting again. A hope to get help. Scared as he was whatever faced him, he hoped would be a solution.

The image of those bodies however kept flashing in his mind. The scare he got at seeing them but the display of courage he did was magnificent. It was remarkable at any level and here is the future king of the uMzingwane kingdom proving his worth of the nomination unknowingly.

# Race Against Time

He was not surprised by what he saw on arrival. He had expected this somehow. Gog' uMhlongo just sat there motionless. One could say she was surprised, confused, or even wondering but she was calm. Over the years she had learned to remain calm even in the middle of a crisis.

She and her initiate had arrived here an hour earlier. When performing ceremonies her initiate was her immediate help and was the one who could translate some things to the people if it happened that she went into a trance and spoke in a language and terms they did not understand. They are waiting for Bab' Mhlongo and his men for this ceremony to begin.

He requested his entry which was granted, and he sat down. A thousand questions were running in his mind. Which one to ask afore the other was the question. He wasn't sure whether he was the one to be asking questions or answering questions.

"Where is the bull'', she asked in an unstable voice with anger underlining it. Confused Bab' uMhlongo did not understand but said they should be here they left an hour ago as usual. He was a ball of emotions as he said so. Confused, concerned and yet afraid of the consequences of the present situation.

"Well, do you see any of them here? she asked and continued even without his response. You were supposed to make sure they get here and on time or maybe you people want to do this your way and by yourselves", she said trailing off in a disappointed yet crystal-angry voice.

He felt exactly where the weight of the world was shifting. Onto his shoulders. The whole ceremony was a disaster and impossible without her input and guidance. She was also right it was his responsibility to ensure that the men arrived on time and began their duties also on time.

He only prayed that this did not mean she was considering pulling out because that would do more harm than good. It meant trouble going through this ceremony and future ones.

He apologised for himself and the men in question and quickly asked for his exit after assuring her that he was going back to fix everything. He just did not comprehend how all of this happened but was determined to do right.

The curious group of drummers and the rest of the people stood motionless. In every setup, some just can't stop talking or asking what is wrong even if it's obvious no one had the answers and so in this group they also kept asking without response.

As this very tense environment continued Bab' uMhlongo appeared from within the forest. He was half walking and running at the same time. The urgency in his speed and the troubled look in his eyes spelt out a very long and sad story.

"The men are not here, I want you to stay right here and keep drumming and singing for you are doing such a good job and I want you to do so until I return", he said and left.

He did that right. Gave them something to do, made them feel important and moved on avoiding any question-and-answer session. He reminded them they had work to complete and focus on so they would do just that and stop interfering with what is wrong.

He had also learnt that through experience. If you do not have sufficient answers just avoid the rising of the first one because from that one oozes out the rest. Experience.

He did not know where exactly he was going. He only wanted to be out of sight so that he can think without the pressures of the masses. He needed space and time to think about this but did not have enough time to do so.

If anyone had the answer as to where these men disappeared to that would have given him a break. To undo the puzzle, he needed to know how is it that they ended up somewhere else which was not the forest, or maybe the mountains had something to do with their disappearance.

As he was still wondering something drew his attention. It was a deep scar on the beautiful face of mother earth with a bull's footprint on it. It meant only one thing to him as he inspected it. Only a full speed running bull could make such a deep imprint??? and so, he knew it. The bull ran away.

Well, it made sense after all. At least it explained why none of the men showed up in the forest. Firstly, they would have no reason to show up with no bull, secondly, they must have been afraid of punishment. Whichever was true was very sad to have happened now. There wasn't much he could do to try and find the men or the bull. He had to devise another plan. Something that will correct the situation. Somehow, he felt responsible. Even Gogo implied so.

He had to go back and tell Gogo what happened or what he thought had happened and convince her that to redeem the situation they had to devise another plan. It didn't matter what they had to do but whatever that was needed to be done now.

As fast as he can he went back into the forest, explaining his theory and the possible way to fix all of it. Gogo had no objections as she too understood how the situation, they found themselves in was.

With her approval of his plan and having her green-lighted the next options, it was back to work for him. The whys and how were left for afterwards. He sighed with great relief and did something he had missed in the intensity of the last few hours. He smiled.

He gathered the men and chose a few that were to go with him back to the village. He wanted them to go and look for another bull and bring it quickly for the ceremony. This time under his guard they were supposed to make no mistakes and arrive on time.

He briefed everyone on what was taking place but blurry, apologised a long apology designed to cover all his flaws... real and imagined. The people assured him that they fully understood, he reminded them of the good work they were doing and urged them to carry on with it until he and the men are back.

He and his recruits headed for the village. One thing in their minds. They hoped to find the bulls still in the village or the minders would have let them go because during this time of the year they were allowed to wander about grazing anywhere day and night.

As he was racing on this bid to fix things his mind was preoccupied with the kingdom politics and how to change some stern laws which made living a bit hard in this kingdom. He realised some of them were too harsh and needed to be revised for the greater good of the kingdom and its people.

One of them was the punishment of crimes or anything deemed as weighty enough for punishment. It worked that people didn't commit crimes due to the steepness of punishment but sometimes there were just causes for people to stray from the norm as was the case with these men right now.

If the bull did break free there was not much, they could have done to restrain it or keep up with it. Yes, they were supposed to ensure that nothing like that happened, but in life, mistakes do happen and, in this case, maybe the mountains had something to do with it and they couldn't possibly control the bull.

As he did, they were moving. Who said a man can't multitask? The only good in this was that he was able to do so alone. His companions were not participating in it or hearing the debate going on in his mind. He ended up resolving that when all this was done, and calm has returned to the kingdom he was going to go over and talk to the chief and the kingdom heads about the possible revision of laws and regulations in this kingdom. That was a done deal and so he kept moving too.

On the other side of the forest, confusion was heightening to climax. The men were busy fighting, disagreeing, and pointing fingers at each other over a dead bull. They were soldiering on with great animosity amongst them.

It only took a word or a slip by either of them for the rest to rush in and say outrageous things designed to insult and anger the other group for they had formed two very differently opinionated groups. Anger was brewing and at some point, would burst over leaving trails of damage along its way.

These people were tired. They also had no idea which direction to take anymore. According to them, they had searched half the forest at this point when in fact they had not. They had been rounding up the same circles simply because penetrating the forest from the end they were in was nearly impossible.

"I am tired and going back", said one man. "Does it mean if we do not find this bull we won't be going back home ever", questioned another one. "I am also hungry and tired, I can't lift my feet anymore, plus it's now clearly hopeless we will find this bull, cried another one desperately.

"Good, because I will be going back with you, if we are, to be honest with ourselves there is no bull here. All this looking we have done has yielded nothing.

What hope do we still have that we will find it? It probably ran too far into the forest. Only if we are going to go that deep, we might find it, but we won't so turning back is a noble idea", he said.

"Are you two out of your minds", hissed another one and continued... of course, it does define a who is who here. It does separate the boys from the men, how can you even suggest such, do you even know what sort of trouble will you're going back to the cause for all of us?

After momentarily pausing and probably reflecting on that sort of trouble he was lamenting on he said, we made this mistake together and we will have to correct it together as well.

A clearing of the throat was heard from within the group and another man with a faint voice, one that lacked life and nearly a whisper said I also won't be able to continue with this journey it's just pointless now. We must make a report otherwise we won't be able to make the deadline and that will be more disastrous than this.

And that was true. So momentarily they caught a wake-up call and reflected on their true situation. It was a sad one. There was no winning at all unless they found the bull or miraculously made it somehow to the ceremony and deadline but that was just a wish at this point.

After a full moment of reflection, another man said I believe you all are forgetting there is a deadline to be met out of cowardice, you are afraid of punishment.

As soon as he finished that, the tall man- Meliwabo Khoza said if you dare call me a coward again you will regret not only saying so but even the day you were born. "Cowardice is not my sin, my actual sin is being mixed up with useless people like you and being expected to accomplish a crucial mission like this one, he said angrily.

Every second was getting tenser than the previous one. Something was bound to happen or give. These men were going to separate or exchange physical blows. Some were going to carry on with the search and yes out of fear while others might gather enough courage to go back and face consequences.

"Brothers, let us gather around, we can't carry on like this, we need to make amends and draft the way forward", said one of the so-called cowards. Surely, they needed a way out of this but that was their biggest problem. They had no leader. Anyone with an opinion will just come out with it and assume leadership for that moment. However, they gathered.

A leaderless gathering seeking to find a solution to a life-threatening challenge. Opinions flew from all directions, there was no order or progress. If your opinion was belittled by everyone you would be toast for those minutes at least until the order retained itself. So, they solved nothing.

For all of them at least this gathering only helped them do one thing they had been longing for. Rest. They had been walking in circles and fruitlessly, soldiering on because there was a duty to observe and a deadline to meet. It was a mammoth task; one they had no choices out of and so the brief rest did them some good.

After the failed meeting it was a do-what-you-want-to-do-situation. It had been a long time coming and it was finally here. They separated. The other three continued searching, the other three said they were going back and the other three remained sitting yet to decide what course of action to take.

Hunger was taking a toll on them. They could not touch the food they had due to demands of custom. Those who returned home hoped to find a way home quickly so they would get food while those who remained were tempted to pick fruits and fill up their energy sources.

The way home wasn't easy to find as was the way in here. The forest was thick, and they did not know where home is from where they were. They only believed that since they are going back in the direction opposite the one, they came through with, it should lead them home.

The ones that continued the search also did not know where they were headed, whether they were coming or going was hard to tell. The universal statement was since they were going forward that should lead them further into the forest, so they continued regardless of whether they were coming or going.

If their film was going to see its end, they were all in for a big surprise. The continuing search crew was headed in the direction of home yet the going home team was headed further into the forest.

Now, the ones that were afraid of getting back home might have ended up home while those desperate to get home were so further away from home in theory and practice. But this film wouldn't let them.

The ones left undecided on what to do eventually decided. Eat and refresh. The way forward was a nightmare the way backwards was a nightmare too so what choice did they have? That is how they convinced themselves that they had to survive.

They even began getting cocky assuring each other that this was a reward for searching thus far to no avail. This was the crime supposedly that had brought them this far. Someone had committed it and they suffered the consequences but oblivious of that fact they continued eating and climbing trees for the juicier lot.

On seeing no storm clouds brewing they began getting comfortable and going further up. When the three of them had lost themselves in this act of theirs and wondered why they didn't do it sooner lightning struck.

It only struck once, and they were no more. It hit only the trees they were on as they went apart and eventually down so did the men. They did not scream or say any last words to each other. Silently they went apart, and they were history.

The fruits they had picked were scattered next to them, a sign to whoever will come this far if ever anyone was going to that this is what happened and why these men were given such a punishment.

Even though they did not expect it to be this severe, they knew they were never going to go scot-free after doing this. It was just like an argument with a train while approaching a railway line, a very ugly no-win situation. The question is why get involved, to begin with when you know you won't make it?

The sacred mountains and or the ancestors had no rhythmic way of responding to anything. It was to be expected that the storm or heavy rains would hit the land if anything went wrong but was not a set or obvious thing. It also depended on the nature of the crime committed and who it was that committed the crime.

Now, this was the hardest part of the ceremonies in this kingdom. When souls got lost in the process of trying to rescue souls. When mistakes happened during the rescue attempts and lives became the ultimate price. It left the people with unanswered questions, mixed emotions, and feelings, especially if it was more than one life taken.

At a point, some wondered if rescuing one life was worth losing more lives for. Some wondered what would have been the consequence of saving more lives by leaving that one life at the mercy of the mountains and forest. Will the mountains punish them more for not coming to attempt to rescue that person?

This was because sometimes they ran around and did so much only to rescue an animal trapped and misbehaving in the mountains. It could be a donkey, bull or even a stray dog. Is human life equal to that of their animals or is the life of their animals worth more? Are they equal? Those were some of the questions that haunted them in the event of losing people in the haze of rituals.

Whatever was true was sad to happen. Whichever was more important was part of a sad riddle. They carried on though in the eventuality of things. One way or the other life had to carry on and so with or without any answer, it did.

Bab' uMhlongo and his men were almost halfway to the village now. It was men against time. If time was aware of their desire to stop it, it would have done them a favour and halted a while but as is the norm it kept moving.

A dark cloud developed in the far East. It sent a chilly feeling to these men's systems because to them it sure meant a storm. The deadline was nearing and if it beat them disaster was going to strike.

They kept moving, hurrying until they reached the village. Upon reaching the village they went straight to the kraals without a word to the ones left in the village.

In the kraal, they disagreed about which bull to pick. There were a couple of good ones in this kraal making it hard to pick one. Arguments went on for some minutes until Bab' Mhlongo decided to make the call. He made his choice, and all obliged.

Two men disappeared into Bab' uMhlongo's home to look for rope and tie this bull. A few more minutes passed, and the tying business was done. This time no mistakes had to happen. Circumstances did not tolerate any.

The cloud had now developed into a big one half covering the sky. Rainbirds soared playfully in the sky. They either signalled that it was going to rain, or it wasn't. Only the old and wise could tell which one it was.

A part of Bab' uMhlongo was relieved that they had the bull for the ceremony at last, yet a part of him was still very much disturbed by the disappearance of the previous group of men that he has always relied on for ceremonies and the running of the daily business in this kingdom. He was still wondering what could have happened to them.

He was certain the bull ran away but what had happened to the man was a mystery. If they were still alive, why is it none of them had come back to brief them on what happened, but he knew it?

They were afraid of punishment. He began wondering if the punishment was too severe. Maybe it needed to be revised otherwise people were bound to run away from the punishment and eventually from the kingdom. He had had this chat with himself before, yet its weight remained.

The punishment they were afraid of had befallen some of them. They did not know what punishment they were to face if they went back without the bull for the ceremony. They just automatically knew whatever it was, was going to be something severe. One which they were afraid to face, and their counterparts had fallen for it, gotten severely punished and never lived to tell the tale.

He was amongst these men, but his mind was far and wide. It ran from the ceremony facing them and the fact that it was becoming a possible failure to the kingdom politics to every other general responsibility that rested over his shoulders.

"How did the other man lose the bull", asked one man oblivious to the fact that everyone was either trying to avoid this question or simply didn't have the answer to the question.

On receiving no response from any of the men he realised that his question was uncalled for, so he didn't further his inquisition and just followed the rest of the men.

It's back to silence again except the silence was broken now and then by their movements. The road ahead was a long one and they didn't know if they were going to be successful in their duties.

They needed to focus and yes, they tried to do just that. It was getting dark outside, but they still could make their way ahead. At least the path was wide, and they were used to it.

As they were nearing the forest Bab' Mhlongo took a step forward. He now was supposed to lead the way. A lot of responsibility lied on his shoulders. The other men were left pacing down to give way to what he had to do before the slaughter.

When the drumming group saw him appear, hope was restored. They began to drum even louder. The singers started singing because they knew his return meant the ceremony was going to be underway any minute from now.

He requested his peaceful entry into the forest. Entry was granted and then he asked Gog' Mhlongo to welcome everyone and prepare for the ceremony to commence.

The men with the bull entered the forest first. They slaughtered it and blood containers were filled. Ululation filled the air. It was like a group of people ululating while it was just two women, an old woman and her initiate taking centre stage. Ululating.

The elders both disappeared further into the forest with the containers filled with blood. No one knew what the containers were for except that it was part of the ceremony. These two never really divulged information or hinted at what happened further afield. Only the two of them were allowed. The rest waited on them.

After a long disappearance, they re-appeared. They never brought the containers back. All which happened with the containers and contents was a secret that was known only between the sacred mountains and the two who partook in the process.

Everyone had been granted entry to the forest and activity had resumed even in the forest like it had happened outside when they were awaiting the return of Bab 'Mhlongo and the men.

While the men finished slaughtering the bull, the boys were busy making a fire. They made a very big fire which was supposed to provide both warmth and light while roasting the meat on the open fire.

The dancers had rehearsed long enough and were ready to do their thing. The singers had enough songs practised and were also ready to do their thing. When all was done singing and dancing began. This was the best part of the ceremony for everyone.

Unlike the little crown prince, they had warmth. They had light. They even had food. Theirs was a tough call but one where you take a piece of home along with you. One which involved entertainment as well.

The drummers were very skilful or were it many years of practice. They gave rhythm after rhythm in a sweet way. The sound was beautiful. The singers also were gifted.

They all did a good job. One that even with everything taking place gave people a moment of joy. The dancers as well had been at it for a while and were ready to showcase talent and skill. It was maybe because of this that the kingdom of the great uMzingwane had become a unit.

Song and dance required unity of purpose, each one depended on the other to bring out the best they could. Much as a game of football brings masses together in the modern day, song and dance played that vital role in this kingdom. At harvest time or any other time of importance to the people, they sang and danced. They shared and laughed.

# Nsika Journeys
# into A New Dawn

Ululation could be heard from a long distance away. Even people back in the villages could hear it. If Nsika was awake he could have heard it too. The men did hear it and so knew the ritual went ahead without them. Now they were even more afraid of what their fate would be.

Gogo Mhlongo and the kingdom women ululated with passion. Whether it was a women's gift given unto these women or many years of practice it just made it perfect. They were doing their job and sure did a splendid one.

The drummers were drumming so skilfully that one would think they were born to do just that. They changed rhythm after rhythm simultaneously with no mistakes or breaks. It was just flowing and beautiful.

The singers had sung through so many ceremonies and rituals they had perfected it. They sang with a spirit and passion which was fascinating and amusing yet entertaining. You could feel them as they sang and you sing along even if you didn't know the words of the song, thus how beautiful it was.

What drove all these people to be so passionate and perfect at all this was their deeply rooted love for their culture. The unity and peace of the kingdom, sharing a common identity, cause and love. Their tradition and culture were their first love and so they were very disciplined and respectful towards the culture and one another.

Also, their leaders instilled strong beliefs in them and were very strong-willed and could survive anything from their young to their very oldest. Utmost respect, unity, love, and discipline plus a genuine observance of their culture was what drove them. It was their standard of life.

Life was very peaceful here. No one lacked in uMzingwane kingdom. An injury to one was an injury to all. Even during the farming or harvesting season, they helped each other ensuring every family has enough food to sustain with. Even those who had no livestock of their own were lent some so that they could sustain their families.

Competition to earn more or become filthy rich and or rule over others was unknown. The kingdom spirit was "we win together, lose together", and try all at once thus they were prosperous as a kingdom not as individuals. They didn't live as units in a kingdom but as one big happy family which made the kingdom and community of uMzingwane kingdom.

Smiles through songs, drumming and ululation were the order of the day tonight as well. It did tell a very long and envious story that despite the challenges presented to them, they were not a lot to break easily. They just loved their own and loved their culture.

As the dancing and drumming came to a halt Bab' uMhlongo sighed, a sigh of relief as he stood to address the people. As he did, they all bowed with respect while others were chanting his clan names and eventually sat down to listen to him.

He gave a speech. He usually did. A part of the ceremonies and rituals or a duty he had to perform, and he did. It was sort of a warning to everyone that the ancestors will not spare any wrongdoing and behaviour which was deemed disrespectful in this kingdom.

Disrespecting the spirits and gods of the land had its consequences which always were not pleasant, so he urged the community to exercise restraint and yet enjoy life in their kingdom after all it was and is their father's land. They were to live and produce in and be happy.

The people took it differently though. For some, it was a warning or reminder which was necessary now and then. For some, the ceremony was incomplete without this part and so it had to be to complete the process.

After the speech and caution, he gave out an order that the drumming and singing were to continue tonight and so they did. This was usually the last part of the ceremony, so everyone gave it their all. The show was coming to an end.

As they did the two leaders of the ceremony disappeared back into the other side of the forest. It was the part where they thanked their ancestors and prepared to leave. It was also the part where they were told by the ancestors if the ceremony went well and if any captured person or persons would be released, how and when and check if anything was needed after all this.

They went in there for a short time. No one noticed that as the people were busy enjoying themselves and having a great time while performing a duty for their kingdom. When the people were deeply engrossed in what they were doing, the two would just slip out.

It went well. They were told everyone in the forest was to be released tomorrow early morning. This meant that they were not closing the shop as far as the proceedings were concerned. The business had to go on for the rest of the night. Well, the people didn't mind and so didn't these two. At least all was well.

It was now all the people because the men who lost the bull and disappeared into the forest were now counted as people rescued from the forest. Had this ritual failed they were going to be stuck here for a good long time.

After the arrival of the rescued people tomorrow another small celebration was to be held back in the village to welcome them home and thank the ancestors for their safe arrival and well-being while away.

Since in this case some were deceased their spirits were also to be welcomed back into the village for them to rest well and with their people. Otherwise, if this is not done, they would wonder about and not find proper rest. They didn't want that because their wondering souls were bound to upset the well-being of the people in a way. They wanted peace. Absolute peace.

They both thanked the ancestors and went back to join the rest of the people now on a jovial note. Since the people were to arrive in the morning the food, dance and song carried on.

The men responsible for the meat and food were distributing more after receiving the news, the singers were doing it for a lifetime while the dancers were not left out. The fire was reignited and made bigger for everyone's warmth and light.

This was the best part of these ceremonies. No one ever went hungry or got bored. Everyone was drinking and merry, eating, and full. Dancing and having a wonderful time.

Soon dawn set in. It was a signal for those going back to prepare for the homecoming ceremony to go back to the village. Tomorrow had finally arrived, and it was over with the forest fun. And so, they set off while the remaining ones eagerly awaited those coming out or that person coming out. They did.

This person or thing was the reason for their forest camp. The reason behind their misery and joy. They were all very keen on finding out who it was or what it was. However, today's revelation was bound to leave them confused at least for this moment.

Dusk was drawing near but at least Nsika could make his way forward. He could still see something which was further afield before bumping onto it. The last thing he needed was for something to just be thrust upon him without seeing it from a distance. He was scared.

As the finality of all the events that had happened since he got into this forest hit him hard a feeling of helplessness overwhelmed him. He let a few tears drop and wondered why is it that he still survived.

Another thought quickly succeeded that one. He couldn't die now after surviving so much. He needed to listen closely maybe the person whose voice has been calling him was guarding over him. That he believed and quickly felt comforted feeling that a powerful being was watching over him. Though to him, it was just a theory, he was yet to find out that it was true.

He was a grandson of the Mhlongo clan and therefore a chosen leader to take over the reign of power from the current leadership. He was here in the forest to experience and see things that were going to assist him in dealing with the kingdom matters and realities of life and the culture of their kingdom, more especially in the matters of faith, obedience, and survival.

He wasn't accidentally called. Only his family had been slow to heed the call he had been telling them about because they believed he was only a child which has brought all of them as a kingdom to this point and moment. It could have been avoided.

That thought fuelled his positivity and gave him comfort, now he could carry on. If he was ever going to get anywhere, he had to focus on getting there so he trudged on with a soldier's spirit determined to get somewhere. Only God knew where.

As he kept on his journey, he missed home. He missed the things he and his younger siblings did together and wondered if they missed him. Swearing out loud; he told himself that when he got home, he would not share any of this with them because they do not love me. They didn't even look for me when I was lost. So, in his conclusion, he was his own man.

His grandmother used to say... "a woman's heart is a deep ocean of secrets" woman or not his heart had to take after his granny's.

Maybe when he grew up and had grandchildren, he would tell them the story of his encounters in the dancing mountains and forest. But until then, he would wait. Maybe they would believe him or think it was just a folktale or an amusing story, that was left for time to tell.

However, seeing as civilisation has worked so hard to erase and look down upon culture and traditional practices or beliefs of the people of uMzingwane, one can only conveniently wonder if they would believe him. Or believe such a kingdom existed or let alone want to live in it.

By now he had difficulties making his way. He was constantly stepping on thorns and wincing at the pain. He tried to avoid the trees, but they just seemed to stand majestically before him. There was no defined way here so one way or the other he was bound to step on something that will make him feel pain.

Even with the darkness, thorns, and pain, he kept moving. If only he could meet someone who could explain all of this, someone who could give meaning to everything.

He needed answers to questions he was yet to ask. The problem is he wasn't sure if he was to be asking questions or answering questions. The latter scared him. As he was walking a lizard crossed his path and he was convinced it was a snake. He ran until he was convinced that he had run enough distance between himself and the snake.

Again, he was faced with an uphill task. Since there was no defined way here it meant he was running while trying to avoid the trees some of which were standing like soldiers on parade, and he saw when he had already bumped into them earning him scratches in the process.

He missed home. He missed the warmth of a fire. He only was left to imagine how good it will feel if he were to have a fire right here and right now. He missed the feeling.

Whether he was going to get home or not was left to be seen for now he had an important agenda. He had to find out who he was within the forest. It could be someone from his kingdom after all.

They could be here to rescue him, he thought. That thought wasn't far from home for him. Except he didn't know it. He wanted to explain that he was lost and that maybe that could earn him a way home. He wanted to scream for help but felt that could be a waste of energy he barely had and depended fully on.

The energy left was to keep walking. He had to focus all his energy on getting somewhere. Screaming also could attract all sorts of attention. Maybe that which he didn't need. The wisdom of this little fellow was astounding. So quickly, swiftly, and quietly he went on which earned him greater chances of survival in this forest.

Soon that strength gave way, and he needed a rest. If anything happened while he slept the invisible being will be responsible. He called him this far and so had to make sure he survived.

He approached one of the tall trees which had a rock at its foot and lay on it. As tired as he was this rest here meant one guaranteed good night's sleep. And so, another night passed for him.

He was just a child but today he had been initiated into adulthood. He had encountered challenges and made his way out of them. He had been in more ways than one tested and he proved worthy of his nomination.

He could have given up at some point or resigned himself to be at the mercy of that unknown that seemed to be controlling everything right now but that too did not phase out his determination to get home or get somewhere.

Where rest was required, he took some. When it was tough to carry on, he stopped but he never quit. He saw an opportunity in every new twist of things. Be it good for him or not he was just ready to keep going.

It was four-thirty in the morning. Nsikayezwe was still sleeping and weary from running the previous night. He woke up to the sound of men talking. Their boots made a sound like that of buffalos in his sleepy ears. He had long been longing, looking, and hoping for someone to show up and help him.

That was it. The people he had been looking for, finally arrived. He momentarily reflected on the dead man and wondered will they not kill him too. That second flashed by, and he decided to call out to them.

At once the men stopped. "Did you hear that", asked the first man. "Yes, it sounded like a child calling out", said the second one. They looked at each other, all three puzzled that how can a child be in the middle of nowhere like this.

Despite the suspicion and questions, they stood and did not move from there. Their greatest suspicion was that maybe the mountains are responsible and playing tricks on them.

Alas, it wasn't a trick. In came the pillar of the uMzingwane kingdom, the future of the nation Nsikayezwe Mhlongo. As he appeared, fear filled these men's hearts. All they could see was greatness, so they bowed down as he approached. He didn't understand but was overjoyed that these men looked familiar and were from his village. They did not recognise him.

No questions were asked luckily for him. They just waited on him and carried on as though they were escorting a king. He just wondered why the kingly treatment when he maybe should be scolded for leaving home like that and spending some days away from home.

He had been crowned in the last two days and the elders knew and could see the signs that is why they didn't question him but treated him so well.

Now that they had found him the mountains were redirecting them to the dead man and to meet up with the other group of men so that all possible questions are answered and as a unit once more, they go back to the village.

First, they were directed to the trio that decided on eating the fruits. And they discovered their bodies and at once knew what happened to them and why. Nsikayezwe didn't understand why they seemed to know and mourn for them but kept quiet all the time and the men were covered up according to the customs of the kingdom.

They mourned them in such a way that touched him, but he couldn't ask them how they related to these men. For all, he knew these men might have died in his presence and he was not ready to answer questions about their death especially if they were related to these men who were his only hope out of this forest.

Since they had been wondering what had become of the other men now, they knew. From here they were to meet up with the trio which said it was going back home. Both these groups were happy to see each other again alive. They were briefed on the passing on of the others and mourned as well.

Now one thing was clear for Nsikayezwe, these men are from his kingdom. They seem to have committed some crime which landed them in the forest. At some point, they fought or disagreed thus why they were apologising to each other.

Whether they are the ones who killed the other trio was a story for some other time for him. No questions were asked about him by the new group, and so they all moved on. They agreed that when they get home, they will present their story as a united front once more. How the bull got lost and why they started looking for it.

If it came with any form of punishment, they would take it together. God knew if they were to unitedly mention also that they fought and separated and just found each other now while they found their other counterparts dead already.

The boy just listened as the men touched on this and that and tried to fix this or that. At the mention of the bull though he had encountered one and witnessed it die. He as pre-decided just didn't mention that he too knows the bull story and how it ended.

Some things made perfect sense while others were just mysterious to him. He connected the dots to some and was blank on some. Since they preferred to call their crime a mistake, he let it be.

Children aged twelve and below did not partake in rituals or ceremonies even when they took place in the villages. Those that took place outside the villages in the mountains were either too far for the kids and with the storms and weather that usually accompanied such it was deemed not good for them, so they were always put under the good care of kingdom childminders. So, he knew nothing about that as he had never attended any such event.

Had he been older he would have known all this time what was happening or what these men were talking about. So, the whys, how and so on kept on piling up for him. However, no one had asked him anything so maybe thus how it was supposed to be. No questions. So, he kept quiet and marched on.

As they appeared the voice that had been speaking to Nsika all this while then spoke to Bab' uMhlongo and said look after the boy, he is the chosen one. He welcomed them and as he did the women ululated and the drummers gave a rhythm to the moment. It was all done in an amazing fashion for Nsika, something he had never seen before.

Now that was a story to be told some other time for him. Questions to be answered in the future and answers to be given by tomorrow. That was a story for other storytellers to narrate. None of anything made any sense but for everyone in the uMzingwane kingdom, one thing was. The ceremony had gone well. It was back to their kingdom now and back to everyday life.

His disappearance gave unusual problems, ones that had them on their toes and his return today is also characterised by things which used to happen a long time ago. Even the ceremony leaders seemed to do things differently and to a discerning eye something was happening or had happened.

They just left the pile of bones there after completing their rituals and never really knew what happened to them. They moved on because whatever they would have gone there for would have been granted. Today they were graced by the presence of their great ancestors and their presence was even in physical ways apparent.

For those who had to quickly rush back for the organising of the welcoming ceremony, it was maybe going to be a tale that such on this day happened. However, knowing the culture and norms of their kingdom they were bound to agree too.

Gogo Mhlongo then started chanting again. She seemed to be in a new state, a state they had not witnessed before. It was like a new being had overtaken her body and was the one speaking. Everyone remained quiet until she was through. It took a while before she seemed to regain herself.

# The Re-Union

The men were given beer and meat to eat since in the last two days they hadn't eaten anything. They momentarily joined their people even though they were awaiting the welcoming ceremony back home to fully mingle. They needed cleansing and that was part of the purposes of the welcoming ceremony.

As they ate and drank the few drummers that were left here sang and drummed. Though they were now weary and not as powerful as yesterday it still counted as good enough for the proceedings.

Part of the explanation was they were just amazed to see these men as the people rescued from the forest because just the other day these men were part of the team that was out to rescue someone who was trapped by the mountains. And the fact they came out with a kingdom's kid who was now said to be chosen one as tiny as he was, was intense.

How does it happen that the rescuer becomes the rescued? It was a mystery for this group. Nonetheless, they had to do what they had come out here to do. Drum and sing.

Meanwhile, Bab 'Mhlongo was busy talking to the ancestors. He was thanking them for the safe arrival of the men and apologising for the dead and asking the ancestors to welcome them and ensure they rest in peace.

Much as the men who passed on had died in the forest it was still a human error that it happened. He still needed to apologise for such. The mountains did not punish any wrongdoing by virtue that there was punishment it was obvious that a need for such had arisen.

The ancestors and the sacred forest were patient they didn't just unleash anger or punishment unless they deemed it necessary. The people were also aware of their way of life so if they still went against it, it did not look good thus moments like loss of life occurred.

He also had a newfound mission. The ancestors had just crowned a prince for their kingdom. It was something to be thankful for. Something to be joyful about because at the passing or retirement of those currently carrying the ropes if no successors are crowned by the ancestors, it proved a challenge to wait on and ask for a successor from within the masses.

Also, their duties were difficult. A person just appointed without the connection to the ancestors or the will of service at heart and the understanding of how the culture was to be preserved or the norms and guidelines to be followed would only destroy the nationhood of this kingdom. That person will have no such values instilled within himself or herself which makes it hard or dutiful to represent the people, especially because it was a full-time duty which requires full dedication.

After all that he asked for peace to return to their kingdom. Guidance and prosperity as well as protection. All that granted he stood up to go back to his people and back to the kingdom from there.

This time everyone noticed that he took quite a long time in there. They just kept giving each other question-filled stares. The staring contest went on a little while longer until they heard movements from within the forest.

When he finally did come out, they stopped the faint drumming to listen to what he had to say. "Thank you all for the job well done. May you prosper and live long enough to serve your kingdom for generations to come", he said in his blessing note.

Also, remember from here there is no looking or turning back. Ensure you do not leave or lose any belongings here because right now we are leaving and not coming back. Remember your respect and honour and be careful. It is most needed especially now that you are leaving. He added words of caution.

Everyone nodded in agreement and stood up to go. He was the last one to leave so everyone went ahead of him. Like a flock of sheep, they went and he as the flock minder followed at a safe distance.

As they marched on, they seemed to follow a particular pattern where a group of young men went ahead of everyone followed by a group of women. Another group of young men followed by girls and then a group of men was at the rear.

Whether it signified something was known by only them. They did not hurry nor walk slowly. They moderately walked. A song was sung, and all the groups fit into their parts. They jellied so well it was amazing.

They sang songs of praise and thankful notes. Their kingdom was on the rise. Their people were given a new strength to lean on as they went forward. As they fought to remain relevant at such a time as that when there was an animal called civilisation which seemed to sweep over anyone it came across.

They were particularly concerned as some kingdoms and their people had seemingly abandoned their native ways of life in favour of this new way. It was unknown what the future will be for them after abandoning their ways in favour of this new way.

These people had a direct link with their ancestors and their roots. That kept them as they were. Now that they were suddenly seemingly catching on this train of civilisation one wondered what was going to happen to their bonds and ties.

One wondered whether it was going to be like a divorce. Everything that accompanies it is tough and, in some instances, unbearable. So, if these people divorced their way of life and ancestors for this new way of life what would be the consequences?

The foreign person who had brought this idea seemed to glorify it. The people in some of the areas who had accepted such seemed to glorify it too. Was it superior? In what way exactly? If so, how is it that it did not accommodate their way of life and maybe gradually allowed them to accept the change resultant of what their experiences were in the new path?

If they were born and existed from generation to generation and all was well why then did the Highest suddenly wasn't amused with their way of worship? Was it him who is fronting this change or a person or even people somewhere who were carefully planning the rollout of such events to achieve a particular goal?? These were some of the questions flooding their minds as they carried on in their journey.

With each step, they drew nearer to the kingdom, and they picked up momentum in their singing. They anticipated fun once more as they had another joyous moment awaiting them ahead.

Evidently, from the confusing revelations which happened in the mountains there were still unanswered questions and maybe some they might not get answers or full explanations to, but they were bound to get some.

Being in the presence of the mouthpieces of the kingdom was comforting because they knew Bab' Mhlongo was there for them and would answer any such questions that they may have. He was the physical eye watching over them and yet the spiritual eye directing their pathways. That gave them a measure of safety and it was a nice feeling.

On arrival at the village, they found the people ready for the welcoming ceremony. They stood outside the main village entrance and awaited instruction. After instruction was given, they proceeded into the village.

Ululation began. The women ululated as if their whole lives depended on it. As they did so those whose husbands were not present here just wondered what might have become of them and why is it that they got separated from the rest of the people. They waited.

Now the singers and the drummers joined the groups that they were temporarily separated from. Singing and dancing complemented by drumming and clapping of hands filled the air.

It was very certain and obvious that today they were doing it for the last time, so they did it for the memories too. They did it so that it will be remembered. So that it will make a difference. They did it for themselves too. They loved doing it.

Amongst these now happy people was a woman who was disturbed by the sight of her son amongst the people said to be rescued from the mountains. More so because he was now referred to as the chosen one of the uMzingwane kingdom. How and when did all this happen? She had so many questions going through her mind.

However, like those whose husbands were not there she had to wait. Like the rest of uMzingwane kingdom, she had to wait. And so, she waited. This though meant that she was in real trouble. Not knowing how her child ended up in the forest was the height of her trouble especially not knowing when exactly this happened.

Before she could get any answers to anything she was expected to give answers herself. How did the child leave home and end up in the forest? The fact that it had been two nights already added to the weight of the questions she had to answer to.

This was the vision he had while interceding for the ritual and community earlier. The men who were referred to in that vision were these. The chief was unavailable, the messenger didn't pass the messages and she didn't have the opportunity to go in and ask the chief to speak to the people regarding this matter.

Now it was too late to reveal what she knew or what she suspected. For one her son is involved in all of this. It could give birth to a new twist that while she knew who was in the forest, she kept the possible death of these men a secret to look out for her son.

It could even be concluded by some that seeing as her son was going to die, she chose to have the men die in his place. So many fingers pointed at her will mean the truth can never be accepted as real and other motives replace it.

Three kingdom men were dead. Her son went into the forest for days and came back as Prince. The ancestors did not reveal it to her. She didn't comprehend why they chose to hide it from her. They usually revealed everything to her even the scariest details of life but did not reveal that her son was heir to the throne.

It wasn't anything unusual or new as he was a grandson to the Mhlongos. It was natural and expected that a son with a direct link to the royalty of the kingdom can at any point be chosen by the ancestors it was just unusual for her to remain in the dark about it.

While this woman was out serving the community as most of the community duties were performed by her this child slipped out and followed the direction of the voice that was calling him straight into the mountains. Soon as he got there the raging storm began which was a signal for her and everyone that soon a ritual will be taking place.

Messengers came in and instructed a full rollout for a ritual which was to be done before the passing of the next two days and her being the pillar of proceedings had her hands full, her mind focused on the duties at hand, the childminders were supposed to notify her if her child was not there, but no one noticed that and so everybody continued in their work.

In such a case it goes back to the mother that she was supposed to ensure and know that all her children are safe and okay. And some were going to conveniently forget the nature of her duties and say even though she should have made sure.

She hadn't yet gone back to her house since the beginning of all this. Her husband was also in the chief duties, so he had not gone go back to his house as is the norm. All they both knew and believed was that the children were with the childminders who were supposed to collect each child from his or her household.

This was going to be a big problem for this kingdom. It might even cause divisions in this perfectly knit kingdom. For her, it was an honest omission that she had not gone back home yet or checked on anything since kingdom duty amounted to the same even more as a family duty.

On spotting his mother that he had been looking for within this mighty nation and crowd, Nsikayezwe ran towards her. He was surprised that she just looked at him when he had thought she will be overjoyed after two days of separation. She was happy except now there was this very disturbing issue to deal with and he was at the centre of it all.

On arrival, Bab' uMhlongo had to quickly rush to the head chief and inform him of everything that transpired while in the mountains. There was also a sensitive and important issue of an heir to the throne who was rescued in the mountains, not only rescued but spiritually chosen and crowned. His crowning had been unique and caused a lot of trouble for the kingdom yet now he understood why.

This meant that they, as the kingdom may have not paid enough attention. For something this big to happen, meant that the great ancestry of the land chose to communicate with them differently and they were not aware. Whichever was true was bound to leave them confused for a while.

When they were done discussing these matters, they then both left to inform the king since this nomination happened while there was a sitting king. It wasn't something new, yet they were to follow procedures in handling the matter.

It served them quite well that all the key people lived within each other's vicinity and so it was easy to go from one place of power to the next. The king who had a vision about something similar during the last two days of ceremonies and rituals was waiting for this to come to an end and then summon his seers about his vision. Today he was going to get his clarity on what his vision meant.

The two were only surprised that as they narrated the events and the end of them, he seemed to already know what had taken place and why. He then instructed them to handle the matter well, introduce him to the people and leave the official crowning to him as he was the one to do it. They thanked their king and left to go back to the ongoing ceremonies.

The ceremony went well and soon finished. The women whose husbands were not present were ushered into the hut where the head chief, Bab' uMhlongo Gog' Mhlongo and other elders were in after discussing how to break the news of their husband's death to them. The introduction of the prince was left for the next day. For today it was time to disperse.

When the news was delivered to them as to what had happened to their husbands the hut was filled with weeping, pain and hurt. That was how the rescue of the future leader of the nation and kingdom ended for them. It left them, widows.

That was hard to bear, and they laid a lot of blame on the mother of the boy whom they believed should have avoided all this by always taking care of her son. Now three lives had been lost instead of one. It was a heavy burden for the boy's mother to carry.

After some time though they were bound to understand. This is how their kingdom had always operated on full respect, service, love and unity.

People came in to comfort them. Everyone by now had heard what had happened to their husbands. Some wondered what exactly might have happened, since no one had a true account of the events, it was left was.

The crowds dispersed, and they went back to their homes. As they did the chief's messengers were going about conveying a message. Early morning the following day, the new prince was to be introduced. Everyone had to attend a meeting convened at the Chief's homestead.

On hearing this message MaDlomo knew the agenda was nothing but to discuss the issue of her son whose forest escapade is now linked with the disappearance and death of three kingdom family man.

Even though there were some general issues to be discussed all she could hear were accusations and could not stop the voices of the weeping women and their accusing words towards her.

After supper and having answered no question at all Nsika gladly retired to his bedroom. No storms. No rain. No nightmares. A promise of a good night's sleep so he hurriedly went to bed and so fell asleep as well.

Mr Mhlongo is in deep thought. He is sizing up a lot of things and reflecting on a couple of things. He is aware and understands at this point that his son transgressed by going into the forest, but he is just a kid and is not aware of any of the penalties thereof.

Uncomfortably perched on a wooden stool beautifully curved and specifically made for him, he leans forward. Whether for support, habit, or tradition a long knobkerrie is nesting under his unstable arm. He keeps shaking his head as if to shake off the troubles in it. It was getting dark in here, but he seemed to prefer it that way.

MaDlomo was still in the kitchen. She, however, had finished what she was doing but dreaded going into the bedroom. In their 20 years of marriage, she had come to know her husband well. She knew when to talk to him and when to remain silent. Tonight, was one of those nights where the price of silence surpassed all and she chose to keep it golden.

After long hesitation, she dragged herself out of the kitchen and headed to the bedroom. The husband remained seated on the stool. Even as she went to bed, he remained seated and seemingly glued to something supposedly on the wall.

They were both very tense and maybe also unsure of what was happening. Much as she wondered what was going on in his mind she pretentiously zoned out.

"MaDlomo", he called out. It sent a chilly feeling in the air as he summoned her, and she quickly got up. "Baba", was her response. As she did, she rose to a sitting position. He cleared his throat and started talking.

"How did it happen that this boy was away for such a length of time, and you were not aware? Now the eyes of this whole kingdom are on me and this family. I do not know whether to hide or celebrate the reigns given to the same boy…", he paused.

She understood this was a very difficult moment for her husband. She let him compose himself. Then he continued. "I do not believe you did not pick this up. This may even mean expulsion from this kingdom, and I can't stand that, even if it doesn't get that far it will give birth to enmity which has not been seen in the kingdom before".

He accused her of many other things, real and imagined. They were both servants and pillars of this community of great importance, much as this could have had further devastating consequences as expulsion one wondered if this kingdom could function without them.

After a long silence, MaDlomo started talking. "Njomane kaMgabhe…Bhebhe owabhebhela etsheni ngoba esaba ukungcola… (clan praises). I hear you, these are very trying and testing times indeed. What has got to be has been, that we are just pawns in the game of life. Our ancestors and the greater being control what happens and is to be, everything happens for a reason and ….", he cut in before she finished that sentence.

"Did you just say everything happens for a reason, huh, did you say that? Now tell me MaDlomo what is the reason for our humiliation right now? What is the reason for my family carrying the cross we are carrying now? How on earth are we to face our respective neighbours? Tell me, why are you quiet now, huh, have you forgotten what the reason is?"

He was charging, demanding, and firing shots. Shots which if he did take a genuine reflective moment he wouldn't be firing seeing as they both were victims of the same circumstances. The man was greatly troubled but so was his wife, so he needed to get a reign in on his emotions.

"Do you honestly and sincerely believe that any of our children could be gone for even an hour, and it comes to my knowledge, and I do not inform you or try to do something about it", she calmly asked him. He didn't respond. A part of him agreed but his emotions wouldn't allow himself to bear the weight of the facts. She looked at him a minute longer and he just bowed his head.

"My honest assessment of this situation is that the ancestors have had everything to do with what has just transpired. You may not want to remember it, especially at a time like right now but our son has been long speaking to us and what have we done about it", she paused.

This was another dose of the truth that he was not ready to deal with right now. A couple of times the boy had spoken, even to invisible beings in their presence but they just ridiculed him. Instead of pondering further on the matter, they chose to close the subject and often warned him not to do that again.

Maybe this was their ancestor's way of punishing them for not listening when they spoke through their son. Even so, he once more refused to lean toward that line of thinking because he didn't want to, but his wife pressed on.

"You see when the ancestors speak, and one does not listen there is bound to be consequences. It is not far-fetched because how is it then his brother who was with him says he did not see that he was not there all this time when they are practically inseparable. A higher power is involved in this thus why it is such a matter beyond comprehension", she said.

"I know it is hard and even more difficult on you, but I urge you to reign in your emotions. Take a moment of sober thoughts and reflection. You will see it too. It pains me as a mother and a seer as well to have missed such important calls but as it has happened, we need to deal with it. It is not necessarily beyond comprehension, but it needs one to look closely and to listen carefully", she said in closing.

She had just nailed it and it was nothing but the whole truth in her utterances. Painful truths even. He was not ready to face it. He hoped for a different version of this. A version more comfortable to bear than the mere fact of his and her omissions. What was a man to do?

MaDlomo was a woman of great wisdom, and he knew it too. If these were her thoughts, then it was highly likely that there was no version better than it. She was a woman who didn't just speak for the sake of it, nor did she argue without need.

She did not speak fast and was always seemingly counting her words and sizing up their meanings before uttering them. She was charismatic yet simple, wise and yet chose to remain humble.

Her words had twisted a knob into his sober thoughts. He was still seated but now had moved back into the seat of the stool. He had been perched on its edge all this while and now he sat properly leaning back and lifting the knobkerrie he had been pressing on.

She knew it. He got the message and for the best, he had better shift his line of thinking. Stop using the victim of circumstances angle and face the realities of life in their kingdom and make peace with the truths and realities thereof.

She did not press nor say a word more. She rose and went outside leaving him there with his thoughts. When she came back, she bade him a good night and quietly retired to bed. She didn't switch off the lamp but decided to leave it on maybe it was going to help him gather his thoughts and finally see the way. She fell asleep.

After a lengthy battle with his thoughts, he rose and put back his knobkerrie in its position. He too went outside for quite a lengthy time. When he returned, he prepared himself for sleep and switched off the lamp. Though his eyes were wide open he lay beside his wife.

It was not a good night for both as they kept rehearsing possible answers to possible questions. They tossed and turned; it was sad. The disappearance of their son had somehow catalysed the death of the kingdom men and that was serious and bad.

It was not the only thing that troubled them. Their major trouble was their son had from time to time came to them sometimes crying and shaken up, but they had always dismissed it. Nsikayezwe had long been telling his parents that someone was calling him.

Every time it happened, he was scolded and told to stop imagining things and being a problem child. Despite the scolding, he would now and then come up with the same matter that someone was calling him.

One stand-out time was when he came screaming that there was a giant snake which had filled his whole hut and it had been there for a long time. When they went to check for it, they could not see anything.

He insisted it was there as he could still see it but no one else except himself could see it. When he finally claimed that it had gone he said an old man had appeared and stood before the snake and the snake started leaving. He went forward and shook an invisible hand which he also claimed the old man had stretched for him. Thereafter he claimed the old man had left with a great smile.

His parents got so angry that they scolded him to stop wasting their time, especially at night and go to sleep like everyone else. He was told that if he ever alarmed the family needlessly, he would be severely punished.

He did not back down from his claims though, every day he maintained his claims. They asked him what the supposed old man said or what he looked like, after he could not enunciate, they said he was just being naughty and that was a punishable offence.

One such time he refused to go to sleep claiming people were standing outside the door. It took a good long time before he was forced to enter his room.

It was largely their fault because they refused to listen or follow up on his claims and now it had come to this. They both felt guilty and chose to blame each other for the crime. His father largely blamed the mother for being a seer he believed at some point she should have had a vision about this or some kind of revelation but truth was she didn't. She was also wishing she had.

This was going to be a big deal but between the two of them, it could have been avoided. Had they communicated, had they allocated some family time and discussed the family matters maybe this too would have popped up and they as a family searched for answers.

The other challenge was it was unusual for anyone other than seers to have visions, especially a child. They needed to listen without judging but with an intent to make sense of what the child was saying. This was a special case.

To get through this now they needed to come closer to each other, they needed to apologise to each other for neglecting each other and their family. They needed to start from where they began in the beginning but looking at the intensity of the moment right now it was nearly impossible for them to turn back toward each other.

The boy was certainly going to be crowned after the announcement of his Prince position and that needed his parents together. A lot needed to be performed and done by his parents for him from not only a parental perspective but also as the leaders of the kingdom and community heads from both ends.

However, right now emotions were high even a little too high. Anger, regret, shame and sorrow while at the same time they needed to be happy, they needed to celebrate the choosing of their firstborn son by the ancestors as the future leader and heir to the throne. As they say, it ran in the family but at this moment it ran in an angry family who potentially was going to tear up.

At least until the meeting was over, they were not going to rest. The saddest part though was that even after the meeting or the outcomes of the meeting they might not get any rest. Sad for such a family.

# MaDlomo Gets Absolved

She was up early to prepare her son who was to be introduced today as the kingdom's Prince, the heir to the thrones of leadership and cultural heritage of this great kingdom. This also meant that he was going to double up as the seer.

There was no case of theft or prostitution recorded or ever experienced in this kingdom. Divorce was something unheard of, differences were there and arose here or there, it was, after all, natural but in the end, things were solved out by the sheer will of heart or help from above. Families were so knit it was joyous to watch. There was no poverty in or amongst themselves.

Everything was simple yet rich, everyone was simple yet sound. Humble yet wise. It was indeed a real rounded-up kingdom on all fronts. Apart from the storms and the disturbances to their lives every now or then and mostly by passers-by and strangers who knew nothing about their life, culture and norms they had a rich life in the uMzingwane kingdom.

The heir had been identified, now it was time to introduce him and groom him as he grew up for the duties ahead of him. The timing looked so wrong. Emotions were imbalanced. People were grieving and some were even unsure of what was happening now in their kingdom. However, the call had been made.

The clock had struck noon and villagers of this great home were gathered at the chief's homestead awaiting the commencing of the meeting. They all arose and acknowledged the chief as he approached and took his seat.

After greeting everyone once more, Chief Qhawelempi Mhlongo requested that there be a moment to respect the deceased. It was a very heavy moment. One too heavy for these people. They were a well-knit kingdom which had a genuine love for each other and so their grief was understandably one.

After that moment everyone sat down. Then the chief started to speak. "A dark cloud has befallen this great kingdom and people, our hearts are sore, doubt and anger are palpable at a time like this. Such times test our strength as people, our unity and our being.

However, this kingdom has faced much worse trials and tribulations in the past, yet we survived. We need therefore to draw lessons and strength from there. Today is not a day of apportioning blame as to who was wrong or right, who didn't or did what, but it is a day for us as a people to hold each other's hands., Grief is easier and lighter when shared. Even custom requires us to", he spoke with such humility yet with great command.

This was key as it helped restore the peace and calm in the kingdom for the good of everyone. When there was peace, everyone was happy. They had enough rains to last their rainy season and cover their year-round water needs thus why they did not exactly welcome or need the frequent warning storms.

Even though the women who had lost their husbands were not present here, he sent words of comfort and condolences again to their families. He spoke a while longer on the subject and promised to have the families assisted in recovering the bodies and bringing their souls back into the kingdom.

Then the sensitive subject came up. The chief said we have an heir to our throne, and it is a wonderful thing that we should all be celebrating. And we do. However, due to time and circumstances, we are unable to go do so now.

We will do so at a better time which he suggested to be four weeks. Since there is so much talk about this boy and his getting into the forest, I would like for the parents of the boy to stand up and address us all on the subject.

The father shot up like an accidentally triggered bullet, clearing his throat, he gave his version of the story. "My chief and my fellow people I greet you. It is with a heavy heart that I stand before you today. I wish I had all the answers to the situation before us and especially the account of how my son ended up in the forest, but I do not.

You all know my duty in this kingdom and it is very impossible that as I am out to serve my community at the same time be aware of what or where the children are"... he paused and then continued.

He went on to give an account of where he was and how events unfolded. His side of the story was easier to understand and so the people murmured in an agreement being the chief messenger and the main go-to person regarding ritual matters, who was next to Bab' Mhlongo.

He laid much blame on his wife whom he openly felt should have checked on their children. However, it was a debatable matter because his wife too held positions in the same order. After all she was the kingdom seer.

She was the lead person on the ritual front for the women and girls. She was also a go-to person regarding all the matters that Gog' Mhlongo handled or dealt with and was the key person making her a major too.

As he sat down a great number of people, unfortunately, agreed with him even though some murmured in disagreement. He was an influential person in the kingdom, so he was heard. Still, his influence part was debatable since his wife was more influential. That card wasn't going to give him a green pass.

Dragging herself up Nsikayezwe's mother stood up to give her side of this story. It was an honest account of events. She was sincere and narrated things as they happened but as she did murmur, and back chatting were heard from the crowd.

"My chief and the people of the great uMzingwane kingdom. A fearless people and the seed of the Source I greet you. I agree with my husband and all of you who are pointing a finger at me over the disappearance of my son and the calamity which has befallen us as a result.

I am a mother and am expected to always be with my children. In the normal order of things, I would be, but as is the requirement of this kingdom and the duties that lay on my shoulders I do not. This is not a complaint because as a servant I must serve to the best of my abilities.

As is the normal procedure, I woke up after clearing my family duties I left the children with the childminders and came here to assume duty. While on duty the storm began and there was panic everywhere.

As I had left the children with the childminders there was no need I believed to go back home but to work with the situation that had risen I believe all of you have known me from childhood and know I wouldn't purposely allow what has happened to happen…

I know a lot of fingers are pointed at me right now, but I do not blame anyone. If this had happened to me, I would have done the same. I would have looked for the culprit on which to pin the blame. I take that fall", she said.

The people were listening and the woman speaking was a wise one. She did not just speak but whenever she opened her mouth she seemed to count and size her words before uttering them. And she continued.

"I am afraid because it seems like I am the only one seeing what is happening here. I left the children with their childminders they did not see or notice the boy was gone.

His brother also didn't notice that the boy wasn't there. No one seemed to notice this, but we all know this boy is hard not to notice if he is around. He always announces his presence. The childminders are always complaining about him even.

A kingdom meeting was held, and everyone was said to be there. In our duties when the kingdom is reported to be altogether, we comfortably get engrossed in our duties. That is exactly what happened.

My greatest suspicion as I stand before you today, are that the ancestors had a hand in this. Thus, it was hidden from all of us. Not even one person picked up on what was happening, and we were all engrossed in the proceedings of the ceremony.

I am not going to speak ill of the men who went into the forest and more especially the ones who have now departed forever but in all things, I believe if we all look closely something was happening in this kingdom and the ancestors knew what but chose to hide it from us. I can't blame them either.

My sincere condolences to the families who are bearing the direct loss at this moment. My heart goes out to them. I am even more saddened because our ancestors hid all this from us. I am not going to hold anything against those who choose to blame me.

We are a society of differences. We live in a way only we should be able to comprehend and if we cease to understand our life no one else will. We do not blame nor accuse each other when the going gets tough. We come together and tackle our differences together. My chief and my fellow people I apologise to you all and more so to my grieving neighbours." Ma'Mhlongo was a very wise woman and knew by so doing she had pointed them all in the direction they should be going.

Without intentionally shifting blame or pointing a finger, she had spoken. A lot of people agreed with her especially the men because they were seen nodding their heads while she spoke. Some silently agreed and some openly disagreed. She sat down.

A heavy silence followed her sitting down. She knew it. It was going to take a while for all these people to make sense of these events and come to terms with such losses, but it was how it was in their kingdom. Sooner or later, they were bound to understand.

After some time, the chief stood up to address the people once more. He said it is unfortunate that life has been lost and so by that measure the kingdom wants to find a culprit and in our desperate need to find someone to blame we have forgotten that it is by the services of this woman here that our kingdom stands.

Let me also mention that the issue at hand right now was that of disrespect, those who went into the same forest for the same reason are here with us today because they chose to observe custom no matter what.

This woman that you are all ready to crucify is one of our own and if the choice was given was never going to choose the death of anyone. It was an error that involved a lot of people in this kingdom, even childminders didn't report that the child was missing.

So many people are involved. And so, by that measure, I urge you all to remember the customs of this kingdom and the service given over the years and every day by this family and forgive any ill you may associate with them.

Right now, we have an heir to the throne, and it is by them that we have one. They are a pillar I need not explain because all of us are aware of it. He reverted to the condolences part and then carried on afterwards.

He paused for a moment, then said let's have the childminders tell us what happened and why did they not report that one of the children was missing especially a Mhlongo. They didn't immediately rise but eventually, all three slowly rose.

They professed complete ignorance to the matter and offered no sizeable explanation apart from that they did not know he was missing. To them, all the kids were there, and it was a mystery that one of them spent such an amount of time away. They gave no substantial explanation until the chief interfered.

He made them sit down, and after that, he touched on kingdom politics and every general thing. Wrapping up, he asked for the boy to be crowned prince to be brought forward. He introduced him with great pride and show of affection.

Sometimes the ancestors delayed revealing future leaders and therefore, it made it difficult to choose anyone to occupy that seat until the rightful person was crowned by the ancestors and later by the kingdom.

This made his work a lot easier. The chief had spoken and made a lot of sense, but it was up to the people to decide what they chose to do. Nail this woman in this kingdom cross or understand the real circumstances, make peace, and move on.

The meeting with the chief was now over, at least that was one step she had passed this far. As the kingdom dispersed emotions were high and diverse. Some condemned her while others were on her side. This matter was far-reaching, and childminders had to be questioned too to balance the equation.

Nsikayezwe was a popular kid due to his family background and his character. He was a bubbly kid whose absence spoke loudly. How is it that they did not notice or enquire about his absence, even ask other kids?

Nsikayezwe was with the other kids when he was called. His leaving wasn't noticed even by the other kids. He swiftly disappeared. That part was a mystery people needed to look at a bit closer.

If they momentarily took a step back from the loss of life and other problems surrounding it the answer was right before them. The Dancing Mountains had everything to do with it.

Now she was back home and waiting to hear from her husband who had laid all the blame on her. There was nothing she could do except wait. Waiting is uneasy especially if there is no clue or hints regarding the subject one is waiting for.

Whether the marriage was going to survive this or not was left to be seen. Whether she was ever going to find peace with her neighbours especially those who had lost their husbands in this season of things was also left to time. So much was left balancing on time to decide. If it was true, that time heals then maybe it was going to heal their wounds.

Half whispering and half addressing herself she said. I know all about time and waiting. It's never a good place to be in but if it has come to that so let it be. She rose to go fetch her children from the outside and make food for them.

# Reflections and Hearty Moments

The sky is blue. There is a cool breeze from the East as the rays of the sun kiss the beautiful face of mother earth. For the last few days, the people of the uMzingwane kingdom have missed such calmness and peace. They are loving it. Given the recent events, they deserved it.

The kingdom is quiet except for the dogs that keep breaking the silence here and there and the bulls making noise at the kraals. Everything else is quiet as if accepting and embracing the calm that has just been restored.

One wonders when next is it that they are going to be under storms again. One wonders when next are they going to be on the run to save a soul or souls. People like Gogo and Bab' Mhlongo are used to it.

They know it won't be long before they serve again. They know it won't be long now before something goes wrong somewhere and repairs are called for and the great unknowns takes course.

They are not complaining though. They are happy to serve. Since their crowning in their youth, they dedicated themselves to serving to the best of their abilities and they are proud.

Grey hair moments are here, and it means they have since grown and rendered full service over the years to the people and nation. They did it well and it shows. The kingdom is proud. The people applaud and are grateful too.

Nsikayezwe is now one to succeed them. The weight of the duties that lie on his shoulders has not yet sunk in or gained meaning at all. He is outside and playing with his brother.

His mother has assigned an older brother whom she has asked for from one of her sisters to come and watch over them especially now that they are all aware of the position Nsikayezwe is in and the fact that left unattended to he may wander again following instructions and direction that they all do not understand or know of.

To her, they were now safe, him and his brother from any harm that may befall them because Methembe was older than them and would quickly report any unusual occurrence of events.

As the events of that day unfold in his mind, his gaze is fixed for far too long in that direction. He has seen it all, knows it all and that is just him and no one else. His brother Bhekisizwe is there with him wondering why he has stopped playing.

He calls out to him, but no response comes out of his brother. He too is looking in that direction but sees nothing but the stretch of beautiful mother earth to the ends where the eye sees no more.

That was the story of the beautiful, mighty and beloved kingdom of uMzingwane and its sacred Dancing Mountains. Some would say it was a wonderful place, some say no it wasn't and the stubborn say whoever witnessed the existence of such a kingdom.

As civilisation has much impacted negatively on African native practices, beliefs, cultures, and lifestyles, only the wise and the old and the cultural at heart can testify.

Nsikayezwe kept the promise he made to himself while wandering in the sacred forest. As his grandmother used to say that a woman's heart is a deep ocean of secrets, he was no woman, but he was his grandmother's offspring and so would dearly hold on to that.

Whether he knew exactly what it meant was left to be seen but today he threw all the events and secrets he encountered in the forest and mountains to that deep ocean. Time will tell.

On the other hand, the mother of the prince is not at peace at all. After everything that has transpired, there is something she has remembered. Something she strongly feels could have saved the lives of the now deceased men.

When she went to consult on whether the ceremony would be a success or if there were further requirements from the ancestors there is a vision she saw. One which landed her at the doorstep of the chief thereafter but unfortunately, she wasn't allowed in because the chief was unavailable at the time of her going there.

She like everyone else had to continue with the proceedings of the day as it was a very busy day. A supercharged one at that. Deeply engrossed in the proceedings and carrying out her duties for the people and the kingdom, especially at a time like this one she did not get another time to visit the chief or to consult again.

The vision had not been so clear, but she did see the warning signs and she did see the faces of some kingdom men. Though blurred at the time now it was clear. What is now troubling her is the thought that maybe this too could have been avoided.

Was it her mistake again or was it just fate? Is this how the story of this chapter and moment was supposed to fold? Is it this or that? The questions flooded but there was no answer to any of them.

At best maybe it was avoidable but at the point she was sitting at it was all done. She like everyone else in the kingdom needed to come to terms with everything and maybe with time this too will pass, and a new chapter is written.

She already had accusing eyes looking at her because of the disappearance of her son. If she came out and said that before the death of these men, she had a warning sign it will weigh more on her.

Had the chief been available it would be a different story but then again it will simply look like she is trying to pin it on the chief, so she had to carry her cross. She did.

One of the neighbours stop by to see how she was doing, and she ended up getting inside the kitchen with her. "MaDlomo, what is bothering you so much? You look troubled, upset even and I hope it's not the recent events in the kingdom", she said. MaDlomo did not respond.

"Tell me, she demanded. How long have you lived in the uMzingwane kingdom? Did you just arrive yesterday or are you a visitor huh? Come on speak up I want to hear it; she kept on demanding and MaDlomo was still mum.

The trick here was everyone had seemingly accused this woman of different things and the coming in of a neighbour giving her a third degree had a couple of reasons to it.

She was not fully sure which was it and she either needed to avoid all questioning or tread carefully if she was to give responses. Or better yet she needed to come out of it and act all fine the best she could.

She was naturally an honest person and a sincere one at that so lying her way out of the third degree would be tough. Thus, while she was figuring out which way, she was to take out of this she remained mum. Her mind and heart were having a contest.

The truth and her feelings and her thoughts based especially on the recent occurrences and the motives behind the neighbour's visit all had an impact. Eventually, she responded.

"It's not about how long I have been here or what did or did not happen", she said and before she continued the neighbour cut in. "You worry too much and even work too much as well. Life is too short and if I were you sometimes I would just delegate and give myself some free time.

One would swear this whole kingdom was given birth to by you from the way you carry it on your shoulders, yet they do not even thank you. Now they are…", before she could finish what they are doing now MaDlomo cut in.

She enquired as to why she had stopped by. It was a way of discouraging her from carrying on the route she had taken.

Exactly why she was uncomfortable speaking to or sharing the real heart of the problems and the fears she was facing with her.

Wisdom asked her to rather change the subject and she obliged. It worked. She then told her some story about having come to borrow some kitchen utensils which she needed to use later today when baking some food for her family. She was swiftly provided with those. After a few more gossip lines she took her leave.

Just as the neighbour left in came Nsika's father. The angriest man in the kingdom right now. Although it was supposed that he was angry at his wife and or the disappearance of their son to whose disappearance the death of three kingdom men is linked. It seemed like there was more to the story of this man.

He seemed to be fighting inner demons. Something only, he could see or feel. There was a rather sad look on his face. He looked once at his wife and looked away. It was like he was embarrassed or something but being a stubborn man as he was even if that was the case he wasn't going to easily admit to wrongdoing. Eventually maybe just not right now.

His wife knew him well and could see the unsettledness though he tried to hide it. A good long moment passed before anyone said anything and then he broke the silence. "Is there any food here I am hungry. Oh, so he wanted food she said to herself quietly and swiftly started preparing some food for him.

He ate quietly but uncomfortably. It was like he expected some scolding, or he expected that something was just going to go off and he was wondering how he will handle it if it did. Nothing went off and no questions were asked so he continued with his food. He finished eating.

She rose to clear the plates and pack them away and thus when he started talking. "MaDlomo, you see it's not that I blame you for the boy's disappearance it was just a shocker to me that you also did not know he was absent for more than a day. You see you are usually on top of everything and even with the work you do you still would be in the know…he paused.

For some reason, she did not interrupt him, and it seemed to make him a little uneasy but he continued. You may misinterpret me, but I love you my wife and in everything, you remain my pride.

Look at how you carry this whole kingdom with ease as though it's no task but I know it weighs on you too. This I know because I am weary in my duties as a man and sometimes wonder how you manage but you seem to manage just fine.

I went away and did some thinking with a clear head, and I notice I erred at the chief's meeting. I was supposed to stand by you as a husband and not supposedly shift the blame on you. After all, this whole kingdom stands by your services, and you were away fulfilling the call of duty.

See I may be a tough man and maybe sometimes look like an unreasonable one, but I exist and stand because you are the wife you are to me. The duties I carry seem like child's play, but I do so successfully because you have my back. I know I do not always apologise or seem to appreciate the person you are and every little work you do around here for the family and kingdom, but you should know today that I do.

This may not be the ideal way to apologise but I need you to know that I live for you and this family and if ever I lost any part of it I would also lose my reason and purpose to live…" He trailed off in silence and seemed to gaze at something outside and fixed his gaze a moment long thus when his wife began to speak.

She did not speak hurriedly. She was filled with emotion, not only because the husband just apologised for nearly everything but because she just got confirmation that the marriage was safe.

One of the things that had troubled her the most during recent events was whether or not the marriage would take a plunge or would somehow be saved.

She assured him of a lot of things and acknowledged that he looked weary. They talked and talked, and it was beautiful after a good long moment of heaviness. As they did, she stood up to call her children and they came in. The family was complete.

They thanked their ancestors and promised to slaughter a goat later in the day and soon after they finished their episode with the ancestors the man left for the kraal with his boys. MaDlomo was heard humming a tune in the kitchen but there were no words to it. It sounded good.

It was a cheerful sound so much even the boys noticed. They smiled at each other because they too had noticed the tension that was at home and the father was absent. Today turned out to be an excellent day indeed. Once again, their ancestors were smiling at them and showering blessings on them.

Of the closely knit homes in this kingdom, this was the best. It was one of the envied homes around because of its soundness but recently had been through some difficult patches, really bad ones such that even separation was possible but like Bab' Mhlongo would say all is well that which ends well.

# Preparations for the
# Crowning Ceremony

It has been four weeks since the ruling of the chief and the day for the crowning and celebration of the crown prince has neared. The people of this kingdom have had some time to make peace with the recent events that took place. They have once again accepted who they are and what makes them the great uMzingwane kingdom.

Even the families who incurred the direct loss have come to terms with their losses. This is how their kingdom is. Punishment is steep but whenever one crosses the lines it is given. Their own should have been careful too and carried themselves accordingly.

Preparations for the crowning ceremony are just beginning and liveliness has just returned to this kingdom. The boys and girls are in the backyard rehearsing. It's song and dance and they are good at it.

One of the songs they are dancing to goes like...

*Savuk' isizwe yebo ngiyavuma*
*Awe maa vumani bo*
*Yebo siyavuma*
*Sizwe sivukile yebo siyavuma*

*Nkosiyohlanga melusi welizwe*
*Awe maa vumani bo*
*Yebo siyavuma*
*Sizwe sivukile yebo siyavuma*

*UMzingwane aww wavukabo*
*UMzingwane aww wavukabo*
*Nsikayezwe melusi wesizwe*
*Vuka Mzingwane Vuka Mzingwane...*

Loosely translated the song sung meant that the whole of uMzingwane has arisen. Instead of reaching points of destruction or end, theirs has arisen afresh. Nsikayezwe their shepherd is the help in which their hopes lie.

The dances accompanying the singing were beautiful and intriguing. So much art and style, creativity at its best yet the dancers displayed so much comfort in what they were doing. Twisting and turning one could only watch in awe. This was a good thing. It was going to unite the kingdom once more and bring peace.

The poets were not left behind. They were also busy reciting a couple of performances expected to grace the event too. This was going to be a very big celebration. One that everyone wants to play a part in.

One of the energetic and fascinating poets is on the stage. His focus and energy are fully dedicated to this, and one can tell his passion is in too. His love for his culture and people is apparent. He is not only doing this as there is going to be the crowning of his prince but because he loves doing it.

His poem goes like this.

*Uma ingekho inkomokazi ashabalele amathole*
*Uma ingekho iNkosi yohlanga siphuke umgogodla*
*isizwe sendabuko.*
*Siyophuzaphi uma umthombo wesizwe usoma*

*Uvukile uMzingwane isizwe somuntu omnyama*
*Inkosi yohlanga, isizwe somdabu*
*Umdabuko wamakhosi akhelwe isizwe*

*Nsikayezwe ikhethiwe Simi ngayo*
*USuku lwenjabulo uSuku lobukhosi*
*Yabekwa insizwa kwavuma madoda*
*Bukhosi bendabuko nhlalo yabensundu*
*Kugcotshwa eyasekhaya ngoba*
*Umthombo wesizwe usekhaya*

*Halala uthi lulunye lwashisa masandle*
*Ngyamvuma Njomane kamgabhe*
*Makhedama omhle*
*Bhebhe owabhebhe letsheni*
*Ngobesesab' ukungcola. Ngyakuvuma*
*Mhlongo Sithi halalaaaaaaaaaa*

Nsikayezwe was at this point very young. He was likely to not fully comprehend what drives these people and why they all want to play a part somehow. Judging from the brave character he displayed during his stay in the forest maybe he would.

For these people, it was going to go down in history. Whatever one did today was going to go into the records that on the day of the crowning of the future heir they were present, and they were the ones to conduct the ceremonies. That was a part of the proud moments of the kingdom politics and history.

The preparations are going very well. A messenger from the chief and the seer's advisor has just stopped by to inspect the proceedings. It is being recorded as well as who did what on the day.

On completing their inspection of the work being done and upon satisfaction they bowed their heads in respect of the work being done and left. Towards sunset, everyone had completed their tasks and they needed to go and rest for tomorrow was going to be a long day. A day where the revival of the spirit of the uMzingwane folks and their unity would be re-affirmed.

A day where sheep get a shepherd, one that will take them further on into the future. If it was in the standards of the civilised of the present day you could equate it to the installation of a new president or prime minister. It was truly a grand event and one for the memories.

You see when events like this occur and you played a part, history will remember you and as the clock ticks and seasons come and go your name shall one day be remembered when the records are read, and you might find favour in the eyes of destiny.

These young men and women knew it. When it came to the matters of their kingdom, their origin and being they were alert. It was a history orally passed, lessons spiritually imparted and experiences internally engraved. It was another reason why they were so vigilant and involved in these matters, the cord that linked them to all this ran deeper than one could comprehend.

It was the beauty of these people. If you judged them at face value, you missed out a lot but if you spent real time amongst them you would be blown away and immediately realised that there is more to this life or rather to their life. The seat of leadership was also one major cord they had and they held it highly with the utmost respect. They believed it to be an order left for them and spiritually connected to their ancestors.

While they were still engrossed and engaged in their different tasks a cloud formed and grew in the distant sky. It started as a small hand size cloud but quickly grew to cover a great part of the east and they knew what it meant. So they began to pack up their stuff and clear up things before the expected downpour.

Rains before and after a major ceremony were considered a good omen. They loved the mere sight of hope it will rain for it pumped good energy into their hearts. It pumped in expectation and gave a peek into the next day's affairs. In anticipation of goodness, they engaged even with more energy and connection.

They were late to respond to the message of the above sky and so before they could pack up all their stuff it poured. Heavy downpours, beautiful rain sounds and a warm feeling of refreshment. No thunder or lightning just water pouring down like someone forgot to turn off the shower and as a result, they were all soaked. Exactly the type of downpour that brought along with it messages of good omens. A mixture of the rain sounds, giggles and laughter as the people ran in all directions trying to flee the rain filled up the air. A very merry sound, a wordless song that touched the heart and hummed along with its beating sound.

In a moment everything and everyone went dead quiet like there never was the activity of people outside. Only the splatter sounds of the raindrops could be heard but that too was not so loud, it happened so quietly almost like somebody had ordered all to take a moment of silence. The people loved it and were gratified by the experience. Their Creator and the universe had said yes, their ancestors had just blessed them and said continue and so they were ready to.

It was in such times that memories of the past and their occurrences came flooding and one could not ignore the weight of such events. The past always did shine the torch and light for the future for they always carried important lessons, not so long ago such a past had visited them and the outcomes were bitter to take in.

The challenge is that a person made a mistake and the whole kingdom paid that price. Greed, self-gratification and selfish desires were the key drivers that landed this kingdom in messes in the past. The throne was always heavily contested, and blood sometimes would eventually spill in the power wrangles that followed. Innocent blood spilling came at a rather heavy cost because the ancestors would ensure whoever was involved paid a price for it and at worst their families too.

Not so long ago a power-hungry king rose to the throne, he claimed that he was supposed to be heir to the throne for reasons he gave but was quickly reminded that the issues of leadership in the kingdom were decided upon by the ancestors of the land who will then go on to guide whomever they chose and if they did not choose you who then was going to guide your leadership.

He had none of it for he had thought this over time and believed that he was doing himself justice for that was what he wanted. In more ways than one, those opposing his kingship were right, if he was not the chosen one then who was going to lead and guide him? Kings did not just sit on that throne but had to be qualified seers who were able to communicate with their ancestors in times of need. Kingship was a key root to the culture and well-being of the people.

The king led not out of physical strength and personal desires but the seat of a king linked the people back to the roots of the land. He was a key communicator between this realm and the one beyond and so knew what needed to be done when and where plus how. His seers were his anchors such that they would be able to confirm some of the messages that he received and also receive those which went straight to them. So, they worked as a team.

The king was not an everyday seer and so that is where the team of his seers came in to deliberate on everyday matters and to maintain the balance in the day-to-day running of the kingdom and its affairs. People could also consult the seers as to their own personal issues and questions but no one would dare approach the king for obvious reasons.

The king that sought to ascend to the throne at that time was neither a seer nor a chosen person in matters of the spirit. That was also a part of the reasons why the people did not recognise him and he was enraged and sought the attention of those he believed would be key in his fight for the throne and boy was he right. A group of young people recruited caused havoc questioning things and people while exerting force in some places. There were very few disagreements in the kingdom especially about the kingship as they relied on their ancestors to settle the matter.

When an opportunity arose for the issue to be challenged these youths were excited. They lacked understanding and respect for their culture and system. They lacked the pride and honour to defend their land and culture but were excited at the prospects of division. The king who wanted to ascend the throne and who eventually did was their friend, and the lord knows what were the promises that were exchanged amongst them if this young king rules.

He did rule for a very short disastrous time and had no time probably to honour the part played by his friends in his ascension to power. The elders met when there were constant reports of harassment and death of some in clashes that temporarily divided people. The recruits were of the idea that the system was unfair and their friend or king as they referred to him had to be equally afforded a chance at this kingship thing. They also argued that why would the ancestors want someone else in the realm of power when the firstborn or eldest son has always taken over if his father the king passed on?

After that meeting, it was resolved to let him have the throne. They agreed that it will be a good lesson for the young people of the kingdom to learn first-hand that when it is said the ancestors decide it was not a joke. They resolved that it will also be a future lesson for the family from which the king is to come to refrain from bickering, self-serving and honour the laws of the land and more so the requirement of the ancestry on whose foundations the kingdom stood.

After his ascension hell broke loose in the kingdom. He had no time to enjoy what he believed were the benefits of becoming king. First, it was a flood that interestingly swept away the royal house that he lived in and he was rescued from the water drowning. No other person lost their life or possession from the ordeal except him and those of his house. His life was momentarily spared.

The kingdom of uMzingwane was known for torrential rains and frequent storms but had not experienced lightning, especially that which threatens life, but it is said that in that year lightning struck constantly and the safe house that he was now staying in caught fire and he escaped though hurt this time. He then moved out of the royal grounds and stayed in the common court where he fell sick and no amount of medical intervention yielded result in his case and so he passed on having ascended to the throne but never ruled.

Lighting would generally strike in the sacred forest at a distance and affect people who could be there at the time, but it was on very few occasions that it did affect lives. In those few times, a person or people would have committed some crime that was conscious and deliberate. The expectation would be storms but in extreme cases, there would be an intentional strike which was meant for that person or people.

The crew that had caused havoc and helped him to ascend the throne was not spared. They too suffered different consequences which led to their passing on during the same period. This did not come to an end until every last of them had passed on. This led to people intentionally uniting around the issue of kingship and chancers to refrain from making claims and or passing opinions on such matters but allowed the seers to do their jobs and the ancestors to peacefully bless whomever they chose and would guide through the process of the leadership of the great people of uMzingwane kingdom.

It was not only guidance that the king received from the ancestry of the land, he also received messages of caution should he be found ruling in an unbefitting way or not ruling fairly in the issues around the kingdom. If he continued in his selfish ways he would eventually get rejected and no king wished to see it happening during his rule so they did rule fairly over the kingdom and its affairs.

An unchosen king who was not led by the ancestors was a dangerous one as he had no one higher to account to or take counsel from. The people's counsel was easy to ignore if one chose to but the ancestor's counsel could never be ignored for it came with consequences, thus even the people rejected or resisted a king who wanted to ascend without the due blessing and call to kingship.

The gamble by the elders of the land paid off as no other person has ever tried to forcefully rule or take to the throne. The ancestry of the land also played a key role by providing an heir while the current king ruled. A system was then devised to protect the young future incoming king and groom him while he grew under the care of the kingdom guardians who made sure nothing happened to this young prince until such time that they took to the throne.

The prince and future king and his family were moved into royal quarters where they lived throughout his childhood and later throughout his reign. If his parents were seers which was usually the case, they would now move to see only over issues of kingship and the ruling of the kingdom for the king and would no longer be available to the general public for consultations. As a result, the next king would or could be from any part of the royal family without following the previous law which required one to be an offspring of the sitting king and be the eldest.

# Nsika Is Crowned

It is 5 am in the morning and the people of uMzingwane kingdom are already up and about. The chosen men for the slaughtering of the bulls have accomplished their assignments and distributing the meat to the respective places where it will be graded and sorted out. The boys assisting them are running around either for this or that. It is well.

There is laughter and song as the women are going about their business. There is enough food to feed the whole kingdom and more. If anyone stopped by this kingdom at such a time, they would have also been fully fed for they had prepared food enough to feed armies.

Today is an even more special event because the King of the great people of uMzingwane kingdom will be gracing this occasion. He was ready. In all the other occasions or ceremonies, the King did not need to attend as they were presided over by the chief. Today he will be here.

King Nkosiyohlanga Mhlongo is a fairly aged man. Dark in complexion with a body defying his current age. Looking almost athletic, he boasted of well-defined muscles which gave a lot of young men a run for their money. He was a fine man. At a young age, he fought in a lot of battles and wars.

When he took over the reins of kingship about twelve years ago, he vowed that his nation will be a peaceful place. He made sure of it. He had united the people in more ways than one and was very committed to ensuring their well-being was always a priority.

However, he was a big disciplinarian. He didn't tolerate any law-breaking or misuse of any position. All things had to be above board or else there would be trouble. He also didn't tolerate laziness, women, and child abuse amongst other things.

The people loved and respected him a lot. Knowing that he was going to be a part of today's ceremony brought a lot of joy to the people. Even though he could be strict at times; he was a fair man and he ensured that the people never went hungry or lacked.

It was not only in the uMzingwane kingdom that he was respected and loved, people from nearby kingdoms and villages loved and respected him too. They often voiced their affection and envy of how life was in this kingdom whenever they interacted with the people of this kingdom. They had oftentimes wondered as to the qualities of their next king but today their questions will be answered.

All the chiefs from the whole of his kingdom were in attendance. Along with them, their subjects had come. It is going to be a huge ceremony. One that everyone from all walks of life in his kingdom and beyond was going to be talking about for a long time.

Bab' uMhlongo and his crew which comprised of his advisors, Gog' uMhlongo and her advisors plus the messengers are emerging from the mountains. They had gone early morning for a thanksgiving ceremony to appreciate the ancestors for choosing an heir so early such that there will be no qualms later.

Now they are going back to re-join the people in the kingdom and celebrate with them. Gog' uMhlongo was elderly, matter of fact they all were aged now but they were all so fit and well. The way they walked and carried themselves was wonderful and envious. What a people.

The minute they reached the kingdom everything began. The prince appeared flanked by his mother and father. They were being led by two traditional leaders fully adorned in traditional regalia and two young men also in traditional regalia covering their backs.

As the king approached ululations and whistles filled the air. There was joy and jubilation. Praises were chanted and so the king took his position and sat down. Song and praises carried on a moment longer and then the master of ceremonies with a motion of his hand signalled the fold of that moment and everyone bowed and proceeded to sit down.

When everyone has seated the master of ceremonies called to the stage a man of great importance in the history of the people of uMzingwane. He was not just a historian but also an elder of this kingdom. His name was Vulindlela Mnkandla. He had seen it all and been a part of it all in this kingdom.

"Whenever I stand up to give the narrative of our people's history, my knees almost give way. It is not an easy subject for someone who witnessed a part of that history as it happened. My heart gets heavy even, but it is necessary to share it as we enjoy our freedom and unity. It is paramount.

Our history is us. We all are aware and know of the battles and wars that we have been a part of in the past and in recent times. Some of which were unnecessary and a result of greed and selfish thinking by other kingdoms around us. Nonetheless, we have also been drawn into such as we had to defend ourselves...", he paused.

The people went quiet. The quietness you can almost feel and touch. Some of them had been there and witnessed the massive loss of life as it happened. Recklessly and selfishly orchestrated yet without warning unleashed on them. It was a sad moment of reflection. Even the young generations were aware of this for they had been told by their elders of what had transpired and how lives were massively lost.

Some who had grown up without parents or families found that wound of loss bleeding afresh each time it was mentioned, but their respective villages had played a role in sheltering them and giving them families to belong in and eventually homes. It was a sad moment of reflection.

Mnkandla then continued…" our forebears engaged in many conflicts, attacks and wars for us to be enjoying the peace we have today. In the majority, we were being attacked and not aggressors. It was an attempt to defend ourselves that we were drawn into such.

Many, if not all here are aware of the secret plan that was hatched by our neighbours claiming that we are on their ancestral land and they want to take it back. They went on to attack us claiming that we in turn intended to attack them with the armoury they claimed to have discovered within our land and kingdom. Their spies were said to have informed them of such.

We know the secret codes that were coded underneath such acts and the intentions thereof which were a complete wipe-out of our ethnic lineages and kingdom, our people and legacy. All of this happened, and we still chose a path of peace and forgiveness.

Some of you were not born at the time and now think it is a piece of history. Some even try to take advantage of that history for foolish gains but it is your reality even so. It has since come to define who you are in a way that affects your everyday choices and life. Learn and understand life.

Many times, I feel our peacefulness and welcoming nature which has seen other people from the surrounding kingdoms settling amongst us; causes them to take advantage of us. Our Ubuntu policies and being maybe our own undoing.

Many times, I feel we are complicit in our own destruction and cry foul when we are hunted and sometimes nearly wiped out. This is why I say to the young generation of this great nation that they must not be deceived, confused or even bought by all sorts of promises the world around you may offer. Be aware and alert and be ready to defend your kingdom.

It is the only land you will ever have. The only place your children will call home. Your future lies not in the promises and the disguised glitters outside your kingdom and people but lies right here. Guard jealously over it. We have chosen a path of peace and forgiveness, but never should that translate to foolishness. He paused before carrying on. He was full of emotion and a degree of hurt was evident in his speech, then he continued again.

Together as well, we have gone through natural disasters. We have lost livestock and human life. We have been down at times but never out. We have always found a way to re-emerge and stronger. We have climbed rough terrains and sailed the roughest of storms.

One may wonder how we did it but for us the answer is simple. Our culture. Our way of life is intricately interwoven with our past, present and future. The guidance and protection from our ancestors have kept us strong and courageous.

The Creator has never for once left us. His help and watch have kept us. He has provided in more ways than one and so as a nation and people we thank the Infinite power and Source. We are a protected people, and we fear not. Even when we are attacked unprepared, we can never be wiped out.

We have always been a nation of great diversity. Our Kings built this nation from different ethnic groups. Today we are one, nobody can come in between us claiming that we are different because we are one. You should therefore keep watch and guard yourselves against such unnecessary divisions because they are planted amongst you only for your destruction.

We have always been a nation of equals; may it remain so until the end of time. As we were let us continue to be, we are also a nation which has always been welcoming, maybe even a bit too much for my liking as other nations tend to take advantage of such.

You are all even aware of the recent attacks that our neighbours unleashed on us. They attacked us knowing that as a people we had chosen a path of peace and forgiveness as a way of life. That we had chosen to bury the past and differences as we move on ahead.

We will not attack anyone but should always be alert and aware of our surroundings. Our peace, our way of life and our women and children deserve that much protection so we shall always be ready to defend this kingdom henceforth.

To our young people, we need you to remain vigilant for you are the future. Study the life and be decisive in your actions when it comes to the defence of this kingdom and nation". He seemed to momentarily pause and reflect, maybe on himself as a young man and life at the time then continued.

"I am aware that there are many things ahead of the programme today so to end my speech I am going to say this. If there is anyone who doesn't ascribe to our way of life, they are free and have a right to leave. Exercise that right for it is yours. Rather you leave for your sake and ours, your freedom and ours too because we value it that much.

Being peaceful does not translate to foolishness. This is the only land and kingdom that belongs to us for our forefathers left this much for us. We will not hold back and watch as our neighbours and other kingdoms come and try to occupy our land.

When that happens, we cease to be peaceful. We can't give peace where we are given a token of death, infiltration, and eventual wipe-out. At all costs, we must reclaim our land, peace and our people's dignity.".

It was an emotional speech, and you could tell the man was emotional as he uttered every word. It was even rather personal as he had witnessed and been part of some of the good and bad that had befallen this kingdom.

As he sat down the environment was momentarily saturated with sorrow. It was a cloud which engulfed them each time there was a mention of the painful past and the losses which were beyond erasing. It was apparent that these people though having chosen peace as a way of life they had suffered a lot.

Maybe that was also what had glued them together. It was also understandable that they had freed people. If anyone ascribed to different values and maybe fancied the way of life in the neighbouring kingdoms that person was free to move because having suffered so much, they didn't need any more trouble. All they wanted was peace and progress.

A good number of women were teary after the speech. Some were even heard sobbing and the men had their heads bowed down. You could see they were in reflective moods or deep thoughts. The young men and women were clearly upset. Outbursts against what had happened to their people were heard from the crowd. It was as if they were itching for a fight.

The master of ceremonies stood up and added on what Mnkandla was on about. "We are a proud nation because we are who and what we are. As the speaker was mentioning now, our forebears built this nation on the principle of Ubuntu deliberately to achieve equality and happiness for all.

Let us then continue to co-exist in peace and that spirit of Ubuntu. It is indeed a wonderful day. One that reminds us of who and what we are. Where we came from and where we are headed to. Praise be unto the Source and the ancestors of this land. Praise be unto all of you for keeping the standards and advancing them at all opportunities availed", he said. A clapping of hands was heard from within the crowd and was echoed by the crowd.

These people were a happy lot. Their choice of forgiveness and peace to achieve the goals of progress was an excellent one. It worked for them. Even though they had not forgotten the pain and suffering that they had been subjected to by their neighbours. The massive loss of life and the spill of innocent blood. The attacks infuriated them but having a reign in on your anger can be helpful. It gives one a sober reflective moment to necessitate the steps into the future. Whatever they may be.

The master of ceremonies briefly chanted praises to the king. The crowd also chanted along with him. That moment passed too, and he introduced the king. As the king rose there was more chanting, ululation and singing. The people were overjoyed.

An *imbongi yeNkosi* (poet) took to the stage as the king arose. He chanted the king's praise names all to the enjoyment of the people. Joyful noises emerged from the crowd with some people standing on their feet. After clearing his throat, the king addressed the people. "Greetings to you all sons and daughters of the great uMzingwane kingdom. May you all be blessed and fruitful by witnessing this day. Today is a wonderful day.

A day where the legacy of our people is carried on. For generations gone by this has been the tradition and way of our people. Today that tradition lies on our shoulders to diligently carry on, fearlessly guard and yet celebrate the beauty of our cultures and tradition. To celebrate our life.

Today is a rather unique day, a time and season upon us where we reflect and yet witness the budding of our kingdom once again. A new sun has risen upon us, and we have been gifted and blessed with a king. We have such hope and happiness because it has been a long time since unto us a young successor was given and we are allowed to see him grow and rise into the leadership that the great Ancestors of uMzingwane kingdom have called him for.

To some, this may well be a little boy but to us, he is our strength. A link to the past, the glorious present and the bright future we are looking forward to. We create our destinies and the Creator together with our Ancestors is our lead. We are a select kind.

We celebrate the crowning of the prince today because he is the future king. You call me king today but here is my king too. You see a man runs his race but at a point should be able to give the button stick to his son because that way there is hope for tomorrow.

Any man with such a son has a future because it is guaranteed. The ancestors who guide us in our everyday walk have today revealed that we are to crown this future king and we thank them.

Now, as you all celebrate and enjoy being mindful of who we are and where we are coming from, remember what makes us and what drives us. Ubuntu mabande…".

He went on for some time with ululations and chanting of the Mhlongo totems here and there from amongst the people." We have come a long way in which we encountered battles and wars but here we are today.

Other kingdoms and even their people might come in the present or future and try to infiltrate you, turn you against each other and eventually even to assimilate you. They may also try to erode your language and or replace it with theirs or any other language, you should always guard against any form of dilution by chance or intention because that will weaken you. Be alert and always be on guard.

The ancestors will continue to protect you if you remain united. They will defend your land and your offspring. The key is to never forget who you are and where you come from, that will give you perspective as to where you are going.". He reminded them of customs and all and then released them for the day. The fun began.

The master of ceremonies called on a group of dancers who left the crowd in awe. They sang and danced skilfully. They mesmerised the people. There was a clapping of hands, shouts of joy and ululation accompanied by whistles. The people had a wonderful time.

It was time for the prince to be introduced. The king was the one to introduce him. He motioned the prince to stand up and he did. "As you all already are aware, here is the nation's crown prince Nsikayezwe Mhlongo the son of Hawulesizwe Mhlongo the eldest son of Mkhaliphi Mhlongo.

He is the reason why we are gathered here today. Although there are many ways that a king is crowned and enthroned, the ancestors chose and crowned him before we did. It is a privilege and honour for us to have our ancestors do it.

It eliminates a lot of processes and gives us the rightful person. It also gives us ample time to groom him and take him through his paces as he embraces his journey", he turned from the people to face the prince and began to address him.

"Nsikayezwe today as you stand before this great nation of people, you have been chosen by the Ancestors to lead and be the custodian of the culture and values of this nation.

The hopes and aspirations of the nation are on your shoulders as you begin the journey ahead of you. May the ancestors give you wisdom as you grow into your position. May they always guide and lead you in the ways that you should lead our people", he said.

As the king closed his address there was ululation, chanting of clan names of the Mhlongos and a lot of jovial sounds were made. The king and the prince sat down, and the proceedings of the day carried on.

The master of ceremonies in a jovial mood introduced another act. The energies of these young people were amazing. They were ready to entertain. They were ready to amuse. To surprise and best of all to enjoy as they did what they loved the most. Like the previous act, it was beautiful and left the crowd hungry for more.

Everyone was in the best of moods today. It was one of those moments. Minutes turned into hours and the day was in motion. After a wonderful time with all the songs and dances and a recap of the history of the uMzingwane people, they sat down for food. Everyone had a share. There was so much food.

There was just great joy amongst these people. They ate and drank. There was enough beer brewed for the enjoyment of all. A new dawn had come where these people were starting afresh.

It was good to see all these smiles, and even more, beautiful to see them carry on as one. The lunch hour passed, and the business of the day continued.

The young men and women of this kingdom were always ready to defend it. They had much value in themselves as to who they were, that value they held made them bold and strong. It made them resilient even. No one could come to attack anything or one that belonged to their kingdom and get away with it.

That pride and oneness were instilled in them from a tender age. It worked well and thus why from generation to generation they never lost themselves or the value of who they are and what they stand for.

The activities of the day soon finished but the beauty of the day remained hung up in the above sky. One could still feel and reminisce what a day it was. The King was led back to his homestead and the elderly went to rest.

The youthful ones remained carrying on with the song and dance. The drinking folks remained to play their part. It was not until late at night that they too dispersed. Nsikayezwe had been crowned and the work begun.

# Nsika in The Royal Court

The next morning was dead quiet as if in contrast with the massive activity that took place just yesterday. Even the dogs seemed tired and unwilling to move around let alone bark. A new leaf had been turned over, a new season had begun, and new hopes were upon the people. The hope of continued peace especially in matters of succession now that this was settled. Hopes that the future will carry them into fruitfulness once more.

The Royal Court is the one receiving or seeing much of the activity as the Crown Prince and his family are moving homes. Now that he had been identified and crowned, he was to be quickly moved to safety in case something happened to him and or his family members. This would have the whole kingdom paying for it and so they moved rather quickly to avoid such.

This was a big change for him and his family. That meant less moving around in the kingdom and less contact with the outside. It meant that his family as well could now only be involved in matters within the Royal Court. His mother was now going to upgrade to only being a seer for the king and the kingdom affairs at that level. If any message came through her for villages around the kingdom, she would send one of the messengers allocated to her to convey the message and what needs to be done.

On the positive side, it was a much-needed break and move for Crown Prince Nsika's parents. Owing to his escapade in the mountains and his eventual crowning some kingdom men had lost their lives. Their neighbours were still in mourning and healing is a process which takes time.

Sure, they were bound to understand that it was how their village and kingdom operated. It was exactly how they lived their lives or lost them if caution was not exercised. Time, as they say, heals and so their pains and wounds would eventually repair but as this happens it would have been a bit awkward rubbing shoulders with them in everyday life.

See, the ancestors of this land did look out for their people. They devised plans and way-outs where needed. Where a matter beyond and out of one's hand occurred and yet that person would still be held responsible, they made sure to protect that person and this beloved family was saved and moved out of the masses into a space where they will continue to serve but in a different way. They were also rewarded for their selfless service rendered to the kingdom over many years. MaDlomo was a chosen person one in unison with the ancestry of this land. She was a hard worker and one who appreciated people and life.

She led well and fairly when given a task and it was part of the reasons why she felt bad about the passing on of the kingdom men with her son playing a key role. She felt sad for them because she genuinely loved and valued people and life so much so she didn't at any point want to witness its loss where it could have been avoided. It was out of her hands and so she made peace with it.

She now was or had been elevated to the position of ruling this kingdom as every king ruled with his mother the Queen. Her counsel will once again be key to keeping the people together. Well, that was at least until her son ascends the throne. For now, she was going to continue advising the current king and doing what was required of her. This was her reward and for those who knew her selflessness it was due, those clouded by the present cloud of hurt would also say so in time as all knew her works all too well.

MaDlomo's first night in the Royal Court was discretely eventful, something which she couldn't understand. All her life she has always been fully and intricately connected to nature, to her feelings and thoughts, but something oracular and unease was happening to her. For the first time in her adult life, she was unsure of herself, she felt detached, uneasy, and even confused.

Her soul was troubled, but she couldn't lay a finger on what the confusion was about. "I am the vessel, the vessel fears nothing, the vessel has no thoughts of its own" MaDlomo murmured to herself. She was trying hard to shake off the fear in her heart. In a way, she knew something big or unusual was about to happen, but she had no such feelings for a very long time.

She was not even sure how to interpret them. "If there is something about to happen, will it be a good thing or it is going to be a bad thing", MaDlomo asked herself a rhetorical question, which she knew was not simply rhetoric, but that it needed serious interrogation. MaDlomo felt out of depth to tackle such a soul-searching question. She was painfully aware that she did not have the pleasure to sidestep the question at hand, she needed to force herself to dig deeper. Was the move to the royal court a trap for her family? Was there a death trap lying somewhere in this royal space for her son? Questions came flooding like the waters of the mighty Zambezi river. She had no power to stop or control them in any way. Her husband had noticed something was not right with his wife and attempted to engage her, but to no avail. After the failed attempt to find out what was the matter, he left her to be. He knew in good time all was going to be revealed anyway.

He however felt that his wife was not being grateful at that moment, he felt that as a family and more so her as a mother of the crown prince she should be the happiest person in the land of their forefathers, for they blessed her womb with a future king. The husband knew that the move came with a status and privileged position in life, he was going to be an important person in the land, whose word is believed, quoted, and lionised as the father of the future king.

His soul, body and mind, agreed with what was happening, he felt so much in tune with what was happening and was so happy to the extent that he disapproved of anything which seemingly sought to disturb this. However, deep down, he had an inkling and fear that something might be brewing, he knew his wife and secretly trusted her instincts, and this fuelled his fear. He did not want to feel this fear, not at this moment in history.

"What if I ignore my wife and we become swept into some sort of volcanic vortex?", he thought to himself. The crown prince's father could feel something in his belly, a tingling feeling he could not decipher. He did not want to entertain a thought which said, this might be a bad move for his family and more so for his son.

He understood the dynamics of power, as much as he believed in the ancestral power in choosing the leader of the kingdom, but he was painfully aware that in many instances power has only changed through war and strife. He felt that the succession is becoming too straightforward and too easy for his comfort. Even so, it was one more thing out of their human control, so they had to be appreciative and honour the decisions taken by their ancestry. "Could something big beyond his intellectual reach be happening which will sweep them away?", the pool of thoughts intensified until he consciously shut the lid.

It was three in the morning when MaDlomo finally managed to get some sleep, she was not sure whether she had slept for many hours or just 5 minutes when she woke up to a jerk as her husband shook her up. He told her that she had been screaming in her sleep to which she agreed to have been having a very scary and difficult dream. She was very reluctant to talk about the dream, but he pressed her until she did. The dream involved her son. In the dream, two male lions were walking leisurely in the bush. The bigger lion looked old and frail while the young lion was full of life and vitality. She couldn't set her eyes off the cub as it was such a beautiful and fine animal.

It was during the day, cloudless and full of life as the birds of the earth were singing and flying by. To her great surprise the weather suddenly changed, from the east came a mountain of dark clouds and beyond those clouds appeared a human-like figure which was said to be coming from the dark planet in that vision. In its hand were two golden spears which were dripping with blood.

When the two lions saw the dark cloud and noticed that it was beginning to rain, they ran to hide in one of the nearby mountains, unaware that the human-like figure was now hiding and waiting for them behind a big bolder they continued. MaDlomo heard a voice saying, break down the spears, break down the spears. She leapt into the air attempting to seize those spears and that was when her husband woke her up, drenching in sweat and trembling.

From that day on MaDlomo knew that her work was to protect and defend the kingdom, but more so her son, she knew something not right was happening. As the protector of her son, she did not know from whom she was protecting him, was it from the King or people from other places? As a woman how was she supposed to protect him or the kingdom? She wasn't sure if her intellect and wisdom would suffice for the mission at hand.

MaDlomo knew that she needed to act and do so very swiftly, she will need to use her brains like never before. She will need to study the political affairs of the kingdom and understand its structure and power movers in intricate ways. Luckily, when her husband was younger, he belonged to Godlwayo regiment, the most feared regiment in the land. The name Godlwayo comes from the verb godla which means to hold close and dearly, the

Godlwayo regiment was only used in battles and wars where other regiments had been defeated.

That vision had been a sign to both that something was not right. As seers, they couldn't afford to ignore such a heavy message. In the past, they had ignored certain telling signs and things went wrong, inclusive of the time that Nsika ended up in the mountains and this time they were not going to take any chances. So, when MaDlomo shared her thoughts with him her ideas fell on fertile soil.

"We need to protect our son", MaDlomo said rather slowly as though she was counting her words. This careful uttering of words seemed to run in the family and their sons had both taken full portions of it. Lifting her head and looking straight into Mr Mhlongo's eyes she laid out her plan. He knew she was serious, and these were serious moments that called for attention and patience, he could tell from her voice and her eyes that she had thought this over and over.

Whenever MaDlomo showed this demeanour, you better listen. It is clear there were vultures after either my son or the king and before long we should uncover and expose them" MaDlomo said. He nodded in agreement as she continued to say, "I am just a woman you know the protection of the kingdom is the work of men, yet the Gods give wisdom and courage to a simple woman of my stature, what am I to do?".

Mr Mhlongo sat there, staring at his wife, and not saying a word, he knew that his wife was no ordinary woman, she was physically stronger than most men and intellectually superior to most, that is why she was so much respected in the kingdom, yet he was still aware of the limitations which the kingdom placed on women and her included. MaDlomo continued "times like these demand open minds, prepared to experience different things, prepared to see things in a new light and to embrace change". She delivered her plan carefully, slowly yet with such command.

She needed to bring the Ibutho commander in on this vision and its possible meanings. She needed men from his regiment to be selected and used in this mission. The mission involved spying on certain things and individuals that may have looked suspicious without raising alarm. If she had misinterpreted this, she wanted it to go away peacefully with no disruptions to life or the current seemingly smooth running of things.

Mhlongo agreed on many levels and gave suggestions that would help the plan. He knew of a few men within the regiment that would fit the characters explained in this mission. When they had finished planning and drafting, he set off to find the *ibutho* (regiment) commander.

Ufezelomnyama was his name. A name he earned after his numerous successes as the commander of ibutho and his ruthlessness. They also said he stung like the black scorpion when put on a mission and his enemies would crumble under that sting. A very befitting name to his profile and history. He was a very well-accomplished man. A proud uMzingwane protector and he lived for it.

He had great respect for their customs and their ancestry. He had great respect again for the Mhlongos, especially the crown prince's mother. It was easy to rope him in the plan and it was in motion in no time. At first, they did not know who or what or where to look so they looked pretty much everywhere until they were led to the right suspect and stayed on his tail. Although at that moment they only thought they were taking measures of caution, they had just begun the most important work of their time.

Her sons were a bit confused in the beginning but had to settle into their new roles. They no longer would attend the same play places. They were no longer going to be under the care of the kingdom childminders but now had their own assigned to them. They were treated differently, and it took a bit of time to adjust to this whole new setting. As children, they didn't understand the sort of danger being out there as those in line for kingship posed for them. Much as they may have missed their previous life this was for the best.

The kingdom and village at large were peaceful, and they didn't exactly expect that anyone in their midst who knew custom, and all could try something. That as was the case the past had taught them some valued lessons that even amid a seemingly peaceful people there could be plotters, there could be some whose lack of gratification might lead their hearts astray.

There were neighbouring kingdoms as well, some of which did not share the same beliefs and customs with them and to upset them they could use the Crown Prince and or his family members to try and upset the present and future of their kingdom and so they needed to cover all possibilities, real and imagined.

His father had been worried, he was upset with himself and his family especially his wife because of the disappearance of the boy which somehow led to the death of the kingdom men. He was unsure of how the future was going to be around his neighbours and in this kingdom. One could say he was frustrated and did not know what to do with himself, he did not know how to protect his family should anything happen to them. On one hand, his fears were understandable, on the other, his faith was failing him as he should have known that what was meant to be would have been anyway.

The crowning of his son and their eventual moving into the Royal Court was something he much needed. He needed time out; he needed a fresh start to be able to carry on. This was going to be it. In his new role, he would not do so much running around anymore but will be confined to the Royal Court only coming out at necessary moments. He needed time to reconnect with the laws of the land and their customs. He was going to be of paramount importance in the event of his son ascending the throne. For now, much like his wife his roles will be advising the king and remaining a seer but for royal purposes.

He was also given his messengers in case he needed to convey messages to people outside the royal grounds. In case he needed something outside these quarters he would send those messengers and they would generally run his errands for him. It was an elevation and a blessing for both.

The most significant part was their relationship with the king. It re-ignited their spirit of belonging and the need to see duty through to the best of their abilities. They were loyal. They were trustworthy. It was easy to work with and alongside them.

The best part was the hunting days when the prince's father and other men who included security personnel would go with the king and prince to hunt. On some days they brought back animals they killed in the exercise for food and at other times they would just go out and not kill any but spend time out in nature, connecting and refreshing. The young prince was being taught important qualities in the process, part of it being the importance of provision and brevity.

The game of hunting was dear to the King, very close to his heart starting from when he was young, this is a tradition that the king created in his kingdom. The hunt is now known as the Royal Hunt, which spawns over a month culminating in the day of the hunt itself. The most important part of the hunt is the days leading to the hunt. These days are crucial in initiating young boys to manhood.

The traditional leaders took turns teaching the young people about their culture, history, family life, and how to treat women and children. The subjects taught are inexhaustive here, but the young people were even taught about nature, such as trees, animals, water, rain, astrology, astronomy and the connection between human beings and nature. A day before the hunt was a day when the King himself delivered his lessons to the young people.

This year's royal hunt was not different from others. Young people from across the nation gathered in the periphery of the royal grounds, adorning all kinds of traditional gear and in possession of different traditional weaponry, such as spears, knobkerries, matchets etc. Most of these young people were healthy, full of life and physically fit.

They worked all year round, when it was spring, it was time to prepare the land for tilling, fences will be mended, and the fields will be secure and ready for tilling. When it was summer it was time to tender and nurture the crops leading to a time of harvest which will be in autumn. At that time, they had a ceremony called Inxwala which was led by their King, and it was a first fruits celebration and thanksgiving to the ancestry and Source of the land.

The joy of seeing their crops bearing fruits and gearing for harvest, they also looked after the animals at this time to ensure that they didn't interfere with the season's fruits by eating and destroying some. The winter season saw a lot of activity which included traditional ceremonies, and celebrations of different sorts. At this time traditional beer will be plenty and there will be enough meat for everyone. Song and dance were the norm and height of the moment. So, there was never a time that people were idle, but they were always involved in some type of activity throughout the year.

The sun played a bigger role in the physique of these young men, they were baked and cooked in the natural oven of the sun, as all their work was done under the blazing African sun. Their brown melanated skin absorbed the heat and strengthened their bones, immune systems and their general physical structure. Their physical health was impeccable and so was their mental health. You hardly heard of any one of them with an ailment, but in the event, they had any, most of them through these initiation sessions were ready as they were taught about plants which were good for healing.

They had a special relationship with the sun, and they took many lessons from it and its cycles. They watched its patterns and could decipher the meanings of its behaviour. The unwell of the kingdom were taken to the waters of the land, spent time there with the seers and then came back to the kingdoms where they would sit in the sun at specific times and in no time, would they be mended and back to normal self.

Diseases were rare but when it happened that one felt unwell it was said and believed that their frequencies needed mending and that they may have missed the mark of their life paths here or there. So, they were taken back to the source, back to nature and went back to the sun then they were eventually restored.

They also had a special relationship with the waters. They knew and believed that the waters held memory from way back into the history of the times of their great ancestors and so it was a criminal act to contaminate any body of water or leave any dirt in it. When they went there for cleansing or any ceremony, they made sure to collect their dirt and clean the place before they left. It was considered respect for their ancestors and higher powers.

Water did not only hold memory for these people, but it was also believed that their great source resided in the waters that is why it was able to give life to animals, people, nature and all because it carried the source within itself. Their relationship with nature was fascinating and if one was to draw conclusions based on their well-being and everyday life one would believe it was necessary.

The elders who were part of this night taught them all about these things and why it was necessary to keep the connections alive. Why it was necessary to keep the land clean and to keep relations amongst each other intentionally genuine and to always do right. It did not only please the people of the land but their ancestors, not only their ancestry but their Source which was the ultimate and if kept well then all was guaranteed to be well.

Today being the big day, the king will be giving his life story which had turned life lesson and the young people are excited, knowing that some of them were going to be chosen to be part of the hunting team. This was seen as a great honour, an honour that did not come easily. It did not only depend on the events of the day but on the recommendations of parents, kingdom elders etc, having assessed the young people over some time.

The fire was crackling, and the young people had just finished eating their evening food. It was a calm star-filled night, a cool breeze came in from the east and the moonlight sealed the view and the feeling was great. The moon is full at this time of the month and shone brightly. The young people are singing war and hunting songs.

*'Indaba yomkhonto, yindaba yesizwe*
*Mfana wawuthathaphi owakho*
*...ngawunikezwa ngubaba*
*Ubaba wawunikezwa ngubabamkhulu*
*Isizwe sakhiwe ngezandla zomndeni wakwethu'*

This song told of their forebears' exploits in building this nation. It invoked the sense of their connectedness with their history. It empowered them with the knowledge of their history and pride that their fathers build this nation with their sweat and toil. It left them with the responsibility of defending and developing their nation.

The singing and dancing were spectacularly beautiful, captivating and inspiring. It was beautiful to be young and full of energy. The young people's muscles were well formed and rippled with every movement, their feet up in the air and back on the ground, you could feel the connectedness and groundedness of these people with nature.

Today it is not only a day for celebrations and entertainment but education as well. Seated beside the king is Nsikayezwe the

Crown Prince. The royal praise singer leapt up and uttered his poetic praise in a shrilling pitched voice, his poem was incandescent and rhythmic, and others responded by loud applause and whistling. The time had come for the king to deliver his annual lesson.

"I was your age when I started hunting. To me, it was just hunting, nothing more nothing less", said the king. The young people were listening attentively and were very quiet. "It only dawned on me years later what the significance of the hunt was. You are lucky because we have now built a programme which leaves no one in doubt as to what the purpose of the hunt is. In the past, the hunt focused more on the physical side of manhood and how brave one was.

These were the qualities our forebears cherished. They taught us so much as we are teaching you today, but they did it differently. You had to learn from your family and the surrounding kingdom by observing and listening. Some things were not explained in black and white, so we worked a little harder to learn and understand our ways. Our duty is to protect our own families and nation.

All the lessons we carry and pass on to you today were taught to us by them, yes, but not in the way we teach you. You had to figure out most of the things by yourself and you had to piece things together yourself. Once you did you were applauded and told eventually that you had passed the test. That is why we have chosen to teach you differently. To ensure your lights shine differently and to intentionally ensure that you understand the meanings in between because life is not a straight line.

The month-long royal hunt seeks to build an all-rounded young person, who will understand himself and others in the community. To build a young man whose sense of loyalty and allegiance to the nation is unquestionable and strong. It served a great purpose in the building and healing of the nation for if you heal the roots you are bound to have a healthy tree and the fruits thereof will be wonderful. It also made sure the young people understood who they were, where they come from, and what the expectation of them was. It also equipped them with the necessary skills to ensure they succeeded.

The king was a great storyteller, he gripped the attention of the young people. "...nature is in you, we do not destroy nature, our hunt is not a senseless act of destruction. If you look after the plants, the animals, water etc, they will, in turn, look after you, your family will not go hungry, and the gods will continually bless the land with the rains and all the goodness therein", he continued his narration and teaching.

In these hunts, the nation benefited from the meat of animals killed, skins for home blankets and adornments to cover their bodies from the vicissitudes and elements of the weather. Pregnant animals and small animals were not allowed to be killed, only the fully grown ones and those who were now very old, this was in a way of managing the herd of animals in the bush. It was also the key reason why they had to be skilled and trained so that they knew what to do once they arrived in the hunting fields.

People depended on animals and animals depended on people, a beautiful synergy and ecosystem of dependence. "The royal hunt has since evolved..." said the king, we no longer hunt for food, but we now focus on building our young men's character. The thrill of the actual hunting event is now reserved for traditional and ritualistic purposes. We now only hunt dangerous animals such as lions, and leopards for the royal gear.

Like I said when I was your age one day we went for the hunt, which at that time was not a national event as it is now. It was me, my brothers, my uncle Mbokazi and many others. We had hunted day and night but couldn't find any of the majestic cats of the land. We were all tired and thirsty, I am sure all of us had wanted to go back home, but you know my uncle Mbokazi, he would not have any of that. If it took hours of hunting to find one leopard, then that is exactly what was going to happen.

I was under a tall dense tree, I could feel it in my blood that something was not right, that feeling couldn't go away, I can't explain how I felt, a bark fell close to me and this forced me to look up. Wow, what I saw left me frozen and speechless, It was a leopard sleeping on a branch of the tree I was under. For a while I did not know what to do, I stayed there looking at one of the most beautiful animals yet one of the most dangerous.

I knew that walking away or making any sound would wake it up and I did not know what was going to happen next. I looked at my hand and I was still holding my spear, a quick thought came to my mind, and I knew it, the only way out of this danger was my spear. He paused and left them hanging at that moment. After clearing his throat, he went on to talk about something else different.

It was hard to tell whether he did that to let the effect of that part of the story sink in or his reflection into that momentarily blinded him with some type of pain he had to shut his eyes off from for a minute and change routes. Whatever the reason was left the youngsters to live in that moment and hang onto it with curiosity and fear. They were left dying to hear what the king did next.

To them, he was like a god, a wise and fearless man, but at this moment he sounded like any one of them, scared and unsure faced with a life-or-death moment. They mused wondering what he did next, he obviously did something brave and thus why he was here today telling the tale, they thought. After a long while, he lifted his leopard gear and showed them some scars on his thighs and arms. "I guess you now know where I got these from", he chuckled.

On that fateful day, the king instinctively decided to kill the leopard, throwing his spear, he aimed for the leopard's heart but missed and caught the leopard on the right shoulder. The leopard leapt at him and within seconds he was on the floor and the mighty animal was tearing at him. Luckily, the spear was still stuck on the tiger's shoulder, miraculously he managed to pull it out and he aimed for the heart. That is how he survived and earned himself praise names, such as ingwe emabalabala yako Mhlongo, uNjomane womkhonto amongst his other praise names.

You could almost touch the joy and curiosity in the hearts of these young men. The joy of being part of this moment. Curiosity about what life was really like at the time they are being told of. Curiosity and wonder, as they wondered what their own reactions and actions would have been faced with such a situation. They soaked such lessons like a sponge and kept them well hidden and preserved in their hearts.

The morale was high, and everyone wanted to be part of the Royal Hunt for its significance and for the experience. It wasn't a walk in the park nor was it child's play but the adrenaline that came with the thoughts of hunting and the dangerous encounters with the wild animals did enough to persuade them to want to partake in the Royal Hunt. It also came with a status of its own, people hold you in high regard if you were or had been a member of the Royal Hunt.

The king's wives and the people around him had long been asking him to consider hanging the boots on hunting. They felt that he was fairly aged now and could not leap nor run as fast as he did in his prime years should a dangerous encounter happen. He was not ready to mainly because this was one of the things that made him. It was intertwined with who he was so much, so he felt giving up on the Royal Hunt was giving up on himself.

He didn't promise that he was going to hang his boots anytime soon, but he was considering it. These to him were part of his last moments, dear moments that he held onto and was emotional each time he had to give such lessons and share his life story with the youngsters of the land. As the fire they were seating around blazed on, a spark went off and one young man's ibhetshu caught fire.

The other young men leapt at once and assisted with putting out that fire. It wasn't anything huge but just a spark that went off with a bit of fire in it and lit up the bottom of his garment. Their response made the king smile. This was confirmation for him that the lessons taught here found a place in their hearts. Lessons of being your brother's keeper and unity. Injury to one was an injury to all and for a moment he smiled.

The other elders who were present also noticed it, looking at each other through the dim firelight they nodded their heads. It was worth it, and the results were showing right before them, and it was well. Tomorrow was a hunting day and they had to go and rest. Rest was important as it allowed their bodies to refresh and be ready in the morning, so they called it a night and went their separate ways.

Amongst them was a man named Mahamba who was key to the hunting escapades, he was most trusted and was one of the people who had risen through the ranks and became close to the king. He was very much involved in the issues of the kingdom's safety so much so that even if he was seen going about at night it was expected that he is overseeing things and ensuring that all was well.

He was a big part of these story nights, both as a security person and as a member of the hunting team. Though he was physically present here, his mind was far away. He disliked these nights and wished something terrible could happen while they sat here and spare him and the other men who were a part of his story here. He was not considered as much and was often laughed at by many as a result of this or that but all that was pretence from his end. One day they were going to learn why he did that.

Many laughed at him as he showed signs of craziness and a disturbed mind and did not spend much time finding out about a crazy man, yet he wasn't even half close to craziness. Mahamba here was their greatest enemy, one that had sacrificed his own life to see his missions to fruition. He was a son and grandson to the oldest Nkankezi family, the Gwebus.

The Gwebu people were the ones who held the history of how the Nkankezi kingdom came about in its early formation days. They also were the ones to consult on issues of kingship and who should ascend the throne. They were the historians of the land and also the custodians of their culture. Generations of this family held that position, their men also served in the key army regiments and were skilful people.

This was the same reason why Mahamba found himself serving in the army and was proud to be one of the defenders of the kingdom. He also was amongst those who grumbled when peace agreements were signed. He felt that leaving the uMzingwane people alone meant giving away that land they sat on whilst his grandfather and father had told them that they arrived here first and own this land to the uMzingwane river and beyond.

His grandfather also claimed that in the olden days as kids they used to herd cattle across the mountains enjoying the fruit of the land which now was sacred land for the uMzingwane people, and they would only have fruits or anything on permission.

His uncle Gwebu who was the chief in their kingdom which was also named after them also fuelled these feelings by openly calling out the leadership of Nkankezi on the decision saying that it was tantamount to selling their children's future for free when they could fight for it and win it back so that the generations that followed will own the whole expanse of land.

That they had failed on several attempts to overthrow and assimilate uMzingwane did not deter them from trying once more. They claimed that times had moved on and they were a different generation, one that was most probably going to win given a chance to do this. The king and his advisers on the other hand believed that peace between them and the neighbouring kingdoms was more progressive.

The king had lived long enough and lost several army men in such battles and was not willing to continue the loss of life when they could co-exist and not interfere with each other for the greater good of all of them. That was what caused the rift amongst his people. Some were for peace while others were of the thought that they still stood a chance to win this battle and take the land back.

Their key claim was that this kingdom was built on their ancestral land, and they were going to fight for it over and over again until they win it back. They claimed that these people had arrived here from where Ngwanes came from conquering and assimilating local tribes and forming the present kingdom and so they were not going to let them prosper forever.

Ever since this kingdom was established and yes on prowess the other nearby kingdoms feared these people and did not trust them much, but they always proved to be a peaceful people that were so welcoming and warm.

As a descendant of generations of men who perished while trying to take back that land, Mahamba was convinced that the past generations wanted them to do this. His position in the trusted regiment also allowed him to partake in schemes of trying to bring down this kingdom even though the missions were not sanctioned by the king.

Chief Gwebu and a few other grumbling chiefs, some of whom didn't want the current chief to continue ruling which was even more a case of rebellion against him than that of the said justice for Nkankezi picked out key people that could be used in that mission.

Mahamba's name came up and the word was sent to these people at different times and places of meeting while laying out this plan. Upon completion of the mission, they would then overthrow their king and restructure the leadership and they were promised key positions.

They were not going to upset things in their kingdom presently but were going to embark on a mission that was going to prove them worthy of leading the people. This mission involved abducting the king of uMzingwane overthrowing it and finally taking charge of things. Many meetings happened until it was agreed that sending men in disguise would be their best shot.

It was risky especially if those men were caught and their mission did not come to fruition and or if something else happened that exposed their intentions. It was then kept top secret in such a way that those partaking in it would just disappear without a trace and emerge in the uMzingwane kingdom where they would live and learn more about their culture and being. The key mission was to find out why was it that they were unable to conquer them.

They would gather information from within and share it with those remaining back home in secret meetings and that would allow them to plan fully and know what to do when and how. This young crop of Nkankezi warriors was hell-bent on making this kingdom pay and was ready to do whatever it took. They had studied them for a long time and learnt that their key weakness was their open hearts and welcoming nature. They studied their ways and practised their culture then entered the kingdom in disguise.

By the time he arrived, several people were already here and would welcome him on the premise that he was funny, and they liked him yet those were his kinsmen. People who had risen into positions around the running of uMzingwane would also influence his ascending once he arrived and had time to familiarise himself and show certain qualities that were valued in this kingdom.

Willingness to run errands no matter how silly the errand looked. Selfless service and open allegiance to the king and his people. Hardworking and rarely complaining was applauded and sometimes left for abantu bokuza meaning those who came.

They would let them be the groundsmen, the messengers and the ones who did all the hard work. A very key weakness that would have easily led to their demise. Some were even recruited to the other *ibutho* regiments except for the Godlwayo regiment where only the descendants of amaNgwane were allowed.

In the years that followed his arrival, he had shown all the qualities they liked about abantu bokuza, people who constantly needed to prove their loyalty with service. He was trusted and loved. He was very witty, and his dry humour had a way of drawing people in. He knew what he was there for and did not miss opportunities to prove himself and win people's hearts.

A lot of meetings in dark corners, in closed spaces and out in the fields or mountains went on amongst these men on a mission. They planned and plotted. They did and undid some knots. They lived amongst these people and ran across kingdoms as they delivered important messages from the seers, the chiefs or the king yet they detested them strongly. They wanted them finished and off the face of the earth.

They liaised with other members of their army regiments who also shared the same sentiments and feelings about uMzingwane. They met with them out in the open fields and often in the mountains. Their journeys around the kingdom were not usually questionable because they were the groundsmen and the messengers.

They were the runners around who travelled the expanse of this kingdom day and night, so it was expected for them to be out even at odd times. This gave them that chance and time to meet with their fellows updating each other on the move to bring uMzingwane down from within.

"Some of you seem to be losing focus here", complained Mahamba who sensed that the other guys were getting comfortable with being here. "It's not a matter of comfort", shot back Menzi who also was given the name upon arriving here. He had been here longer than all of them. After clearing his throat, he continued...

"It has been years that some of us have lived here, it is also a bit unlikely that we will succeed in this mission, you live here now, you know these people and their gods and am sure you understand why our forebears were dealt the cards they were played in trying such a thing.

Secondly, you cannot help but fall in love with the people here, they are genuine and simple, yes, they came from wherever they did who didn't? We all migrated for this reason or that and here we are as well, think about that", he said.

He had a point, one they all at some point battled with. The warmth of the people of uMzingwane, their genuine love even though their reference to people who joined their kingdom at will as *abantu bokuza* (those who came later) was a bit sour, they still had good hearts. Their ancestry key as it was in everything was probably giving them a long rope with which they would hang themselves one day. All these were facts in their faces, slowly taking the mojo out of their missions but as promised they were here to complete the mission, which they thinly hung onto.

Mahamba was fresh, he was the last one to get here and it infuriated him to see his people getting soft and considerate. They were not here to consider or even to think, they had thought this out many times back home and in their planning meetings. "No, I refuse to be roped into those weak thoughts he barked, we will see this through, and I will make sure of it, besides even if you go soft now if these people discovered your true identities they would kill you, it's better to die for the mission than against it", he said.

"We need to find a way to lure the king and that crown prince of theirs into the woods and abduct them. I would find much pleasure in killing them myself but some of his men will be present so that won't be possible, he paused as though to reflect on the joy it would give him to personally kill the two.

In that silence Zenzo cut in, you are so right, that could be our final way out. We will let the other team from home do the abducting and you play along as victims. Once it is done then we will meet and organise a terror rain in the kingdom", he excitedly said. Menzi laughed out loud at this idea and the excitement that followed it. He composed himself and began to speak.

"You speak as though you have not lived in this place long enough. Have you forgotten about Fezela and his Godlwayo regiment? Once they pick up on such activity, we might not even make it to the terror planning meeting you are talking about", he said. The sting of that regiment left nothing breathing once they began to move in a battle what more of such a small group of men, but they were determined and refused to let the truth lead them.

"We will have to move fast such that by the time they pick up on this it will be too late", cut in Mahamba. He was afraid of the Godlwayo regiment and especially its commander but had come too far to give up and go back home empty-handed, so he pressed on.

They all missed home anyway. Their families believed that they may have died a long time ago since they left home with no word of where they were going or when they were coming back. He wanted to go back as a hero. He desperately wanted to prove a point and wanted to turn victor somehow after all these decades.

By the look of things, their families did not know they were still alive. Their kingdom rulers and the king were not aware of this plan and its intended outcomes. There were a few chiefs who knew and kept it top secret and a few men that were directly involved in this so it was imperative that they win so that even those who were not aware of all this will crown them as heroes and give due praise to such intelligent and selfless service to their kingdom.

In the end, the plan was to abduct the king and crown prince to upset this kingdom. When that was done even Fezela and his men will not know what hit them. It will give them an upper hand in everything that will follow. The plan was finalised largely on Mahamba's impatience and iron heart.

The other man seemed to now follow but at a distance, they were exhausted and doubtful that this will end well. The fibre that kept them going was the thought that it was served to their people, the very reason they came this far in the first place they went along with the plan.

Theirs was to gather information, to learn as much and get involved as much to know that which the everyday men did not know. Theirs was a long-time service and they had done that well. This was now Mahamba's show as he was the one to see to the abduction of the key people in the kingdom and lead them into the steps, they were to take next. They went back into the kingdom and waited.

# Mahamba the Mole

This kingdom darling was named Mahamba after the way he arrived in the kingdom. One day he just appeared and seemed a little confused and the people thought maybe he was confused by their way of life. He confessed to have been walking around and not knowing where his original home was. The people called him Mahamba because he could not remember his name, a name that stuck with him henceforth.

As a norm if you arrived in uMzingwane and for some reason wanted to stay you were allowed to. In the days that followed his arrival, he proved to be a hard worker and people began to take a liking to him. He seemed to gain more and more of his reasoning capacity and began to act more normal around people and it was concluded that his loss of memory and confusion may have been resultant of going around a lot and he was offered a place to stay and thus how he joined these mighty people and became one of their own.

He quickly grew into the culture and practises of these people so much, so it became difficult to differentiate between him and the locals by blood and birth. His case was not peculiar though because several people had joined this community by will and by fascination. Some got charmed and marvelled at their ways of doing things, their kingdom and nature. Everything around uMzingwane had a way of drawing you in somehow. The kingdom was beautiful.

Owing to his hardworking nature and easiness Mahamba quickly became one of the important people in this kingdom and particularly in this village. First off, he became a messenger for the seers of the land rising in rank to become a messenger for the chief. He stayed in that position for a while and then he was selected to become one of the security personnel around the Royal Court and most importantly around the king.

He remained humble and proved to be selfless in his discharging of duty and was always efficient and effective in whatever was trusted in his hands. The king could send him on important missions alone knowing fully well that he will execute and come back victorious. Sent alongside other men he would be trusted to oversee the process. That was how much he was trusted in the kingdom and the kingdom's affairs.

To MaDlomo however, there was always something amiss and off about his character. Whenever he was close to or around MaDlomo he also would scurry off hurrying into oblivion. He always seemed uneasy around her, but a lot of people were.

She had tried to raise the subject of this man either with her husband, with other seers or with the chief but none seemed to see anything wrong with him, a matter of fact they just saw a godsend, someone who lost his way and ended up with them and amongst them selflessly carrying the difficult tasks around the kingdom.

At one point again she tried to raise the issue with the chief enquiring as to why he was given such duties and positions rather quickly without vetting and or spiritual consultations, the chief dismissed it saying if he was meant to be trouble by now, he would have shown his true colours but he had remained loyal and genuine so it was only fair to reward his hard work and loyalty. In the end, she left the matter alone. Their paths did not constantly cross anyway so she continued her way, and he did the same.

Now that she was in the Royal Court their paths were constantly crossing and that feeling returned to MaDlomo but because she had tried to raise this issue in the past, she decided to let it be but find her ways of proving herself wrong on the matter. This one was not a matter of spirit for her, it was a matter of intelligence. She did not consult about it but watched the man closely. He put two of the men in her service on his tail and asked for it to remain top secret.

If she was right, they would save the kingdom from some kind of trouble which could befall them if they continued to be too trusting and let things be. If she was wrong and it was just their vibrations which didn't link well, she didn't want to soil his name and maybe cause a bit of unrest. She had to be wise about it and lo she was one wise being and so she continued cautiously.

Interestingly, as if he was sensing what was happening, he also began to not frequent the Royal Court. In some instances, he would delegate duties to the man below him to avoid meeting with her. That alone fuelled her suspicions. She did not live in the Royal Court before but fairly believed that those concerned with the security and well-being of this very important place needed to be here frequently doing duty and ensuring this or that.

The king did not see it as a telling sign because he had men below him and it was his right and decision to delegate where he felt the need to and so life continued in the kingdom. The men tasked with following his on and off-duty activity were busy collecting information and bringing it to MaDlomo by day.

Sometimes they followed him into the darkness of night to the mountain side. He was seen meeting with men they could not identify at first because they had to maintain distance or risk being seen. This could have led to their deaths seeing they were outnumbered.

These men climbed the mountain from the other side risking it all to appear on the other side and meet with Mahamba who gave them vital information and the current affairs of the kingdom. In one of the meetings, he was overheard asking the other men to organise rather quickly and work on what they already have because things have changed, and that woman is now in the Royal Court which might interfere with their mission.

On the other meeting, he was overheard bemoaning their lack of speed in executing and lamenting the presence of that woman, which was making things difficult, he confessed to being afraid of going to the royal grounds lately because she seemed to see through him.

All this evidence was what MaDlomo needed but had no way to approach the king with such information. She kept it as they continued to dig further. Fezela and his men were also on the tail of these men and so there was no need to panic so she kept her cool. Information continued to be shared amongst Fezela, his men and Mhlongo and his family.

He came here feigning loss of memory and a lost mind which is exactly what had happened to their people on several occasions when they fought against uMzingwane. They failed to read it and further made a mess of things by not questioning why the man quickly returned to normalcy except for not remembering his name. He did that deliberately for if he told them his name they would have known where he came from and maybe suspected him.

That was genius of him, and it worked right in his favour. His hard work and selflessness were aimed at recognition, and it came exactly as he planned. Rising through the ranks of power gave him the much-needed opportunity to be as close as possible to the ruling of this kingdom and its most guarded secrets, its roots and core and well they played right into his hands and positioned him there.

The only challenge was the network of this kingdom was tight and it was not easy to just strike even from within. He now also believed that the ancestors of these people were truly brutal and moved rather swiftly and in unpredictable ways so it was not easy to foretell what will happen if you did anything.

You would expect the other and yet the other completely different happened. The crowning of the Prince and the move by his family into the Royal Court also upset things, it undid a good part of the work he had done for a long time.

Now he needed to move fast, or he was going to be forever trapped amongst a people he loathed. A people he held accountable for what happened to his grandfather, father and uncle for they all were in the king's service at the time. A people he had absolutely no respect for, but fear kept him in check. Hope that one day his mission of bringing this kingdom down from within will materialise kept him going. The new developments upset his momentum.

Their meetings in the mountains had been constant throughout the years and sometimes he crossed the mountains going home for a moment and quickly returning so that he doesn't get caught. He had promised his people to stay patient because he was about to do justice.

Justice that history will always kneel remembering. Justice that will lift their kingdom such that each time it was spoken of whether now or in the future it will be spoken of with reverence and respect. Justice that he needed the most to be able to return home. Since this was an unsanctioned mission, they badly needed to succeed, or their troubles would double.

Fezela and his men were gathering information about their movements and intentions, comparing notes with what MaDlomo's spy men had gathered and said about these men. It matched perfectly. Piecing the puzzle bit by bit and nearing its completion day by day they silently went on their missions. Life on the other hand was continuing normal for the kingdom and its people. No one suspected anything of anybody, and all was well.

When the army men got too involved the spy men returned to their positions of the everyday running other errands for MaDlomo. They were aware that something potentially huge was going to befall their kingdom and hoping only for the best. They also had the utmost faith in the abilities of the Godlwayo regiment, so they safely moved away from the mission yet with curious eyes they went on with life.

The plan for Mahamba and his men was simple. They would abduct the king and the prince together at once while out on hunting missions. Having taken both the sitting and prospective king they would then rain terror on this kingdom which would have suffered a double blow.

He knew that installing a king was not an easy process from experience. He knew that a prince stolen was hard to replace especially if it was not a prince by blood or birth but by call and choice of the ancestors. He knew far too much and was convinced this was the best way to deal with these people.

The king will be very hard to replace in an instant, a prince was even far much harder to get for they would have to wait for a word of direction which no one could place a timeframe. Even if they did manage to put in a replacement, he knew it wouldn't be the same.

These people loved their culture, apart from the scary bits about their customs they adored their ancestry and way of life. If you are upset that you would have most probably broken them for a good long time. He knew it, he had spent time amongst them, learning, finding out and passing information to his men who in turn passed it to their rulers. Whether he told them all word for word was a confirmation the future was going to give for now the focus was on bringing down the uMzingwane kingdom and upsetting its core codes of existence.

Fezela's men followed him into a meeting which was held in a different place. This was where they hunted with the king. He was seen showing them things with his hands, pointing in this or that direction in what could have been a mock session of how to do what needed to be done.

They later sat down behind some bushes which allowed the men to come closer and hear what was being said. Mahamba was telling the men that they should not make any mistake but capture both the king and prince and cross over to their home with them. He was giving them a word of caution reminding them that this was a top-secret mission. One which people were not aware of and they needed to be cautious even after capturing the two.

He was going to be submissive, and act surprised at their attack. As the key person that would allow them time to escape. The meeting ended with the men mumbling a chant mockingly saying... hail you oh Mzingwane here is to your last breath., they laughed triumphantly and parted ways. Mahamba who moved very swift and quiet headed back to his house and woke up as though nothing had happened.

The ground was set, and the games were about to begin as MaDlomo watched with a curious and careful eye. Her husband was also kept on his toes by what was happening especially because he spent time around the king. He wished that he could let him in on the secret but was not sure how that was going to affect the mission at hand. He had been in this regiment before and knew that it was a very effective regiment and one which boasted of good army men, skilled and experienced. Whatever Mahamba's plan would be foiled in no time.

He worried about a lot of things lately. The kingdom's safety, if men could come from that far and live amongst them for years without them picking it up then they were in real danger and needed to revise several things concerning security. He was worried about his son's well-being.

It would be a good long time before he sat on the throne, yet even before then in his teens' danger lurked for him. He tried to look through the years that followed before his son ascended the throne and realised a heavy-duty lay on his shoulders.

His primary duty was to protect him as his son and crown prince. Under the same breath, his thoughts drifted to the king. He was unsafe in his kingdom. He was unsafe in a place he oversaw, where he commanded things yet under his command were his biggest foes.

He felt quite sad for him and realised that it truly was not easy to lead. The king had a good heart and a sound mind. He judged well but seemingly missed some marks as it stands now. Who could be more perfect than he was? Would his son make a better king? What kind of king was he going to be? Would their people be proud of him as they are of the current king? Thoughts flooded his ageing mind and he felt so tired, yet it was the most important time of his life. One where his focus and judgement will be key in some things.

The plan today was to delay the king and prince in their hunting mission. Fezela had said that they needed to allow his men to go before the king and his men. They would either follow the incoming men to a place where they would then capture them.

When that was done, they would keep them there until the king and his hunting team arrived which would also give them a moment to capture Mahamba who was the inside men then bring back all of them to the Royal Court for the judgement of their case.

MaDlomo went in to see the king with some urgent information that he couldn't afford to let pass. The king sent one of his messengers to tell the men to wait where they were he would be joining them soon. She had also told those preparing the prince for the journey to slow down and only release him when she had come back.

They obliged and waited for her. Mahamba was so frustrated with the delay so much that he was seen pacing up and down until she emerged from within the king's quarters. She greeted him and he nodded as he observed her presence, but the impatience was apparent.

She went on to release the prince for the hunt and his father was also complaining that she took a bit longer. She responded to him by saying what must happen is happening, the hunt will be forgotten but the day's event was to bring an eternal change. He knew exactly what she meant by that, and the weight of those words seemed to awaken him even more to how dangerous today was.

Mahamba had a frustrating pace which was noticed by all, but they just thought maybe it was resultant of the delays and that it will soon be noon. Mhlongo observed him closely and could see his discomfort and frustration emanating from not just the noon that was approaching but something bigger. He knew exactly what that was, and he began to marvel at his wife's intelligence. A woman who managed to pick this up where everyone couldn't. She was truly a gift to this kingdom. As they trekked on, he wondered if the people of this kingdom knew how lucky they were to have her.

Fezela and the men that had gone before the hunting team were experienced in matters of war. They were trusted army men and a camp that had never been defeated in any battle. They ransacked the mountainside in search of anybody there and picked up a trail of men who wore dark green to camouflage.

There were a good number of them, and they needed to act with wisdom and caution to be able to overpower them. The idea was not to spill blood but to take them alive back to the kingdom.

They quickly moved and caught up with them as they positioned themselves in the area that Mahamba had shown them and promised that he would intentionally take the king hunting in that same position.

When they were settled and lying in wait ready to pounce when the signal was given, the army men moved in with stealth and precision. In no time they had been rounded up and caught except for two who managed to break away and run, even so, their running would not yield much as there was no easy way out especially if you had men in pursuit.

The king and his subjects finally arrived at this place where Mahamba had said he observed an ingwe and noticed that a group of impalas also grazed and or passed through on their way to drink. He positioned the other men leaving him with the prince's father, king and prince at a position he said would be easier to spot the animals coming through. He also said in case they missed the other men positioned on either side will be able to finish off the mission. It sounded like a perfect plan, and they all stood there in wait.

After a good long wait, the king decided they move on or it was going to be noon and hot without doing anything. Mahamba insisted they wait maybe the impalas were delayed or something. While they were still arguing on whether to wait or move on the impalas arrived, but did in human form and captivity. Mahamba attempted to run but was quickly blocked and stopped. Operation destroy uMzingwane kingdom had once more failed and they survived. One more lesson for the future.

The king had over the years trained himself to reign in on his temper so that he would see clearly and judge fairly but today he was enraged. The journey back to the royal grounds was short. The heat of the sun was not felt. All except Nsikayezwe were furious. He was rather annoyed that these guys interrupted their hunt, the elders and the future were going to clearly paint the meanings of the occasions of today for him.

The captured men and the army men sat at the king's Indaba while the king, prince and his father proceeded to the Royal Court. The king had seen many things in his life, but this was the height of things. He had read many situations at a distance and successfully carried out missions, today spoke back to him in sad tones and he needed to be left alone for a while.

The other inside men that worked with Mahamba were known as they had been observed on several occasions meeting and planning together. Messengers were sent to go and bring them into the same place as Mahamba and others.

The men had panicked and went into hiding waiting for the news of whether the mission was successful. In uMzingwane you could only run so far but not hide. They were eventually apprehended heading towards the mountains where they either hoped to stay in wait and see the results or cross over and run back to their kingdom.

Running back into their kingdom wasn't easy without information on how the affairs of the day went. "Maybe we should have waited for Mahamba's return before deciding to run", said Zenzo when they finally rested under a huge Amarula tree. They were exhausted and were not sure whether to engage in a full flight or trek back.

"I think we did the right thing", Menzi assured him and his fellows before continuing, "uMzingwane people are fairly nice but remember their ruthlessness when prompted, we do not know how the mission went but are certain it happened as all systems were in place, if it failed for some reason we would have been toast before we could ask Mahamba what happened and why did the mission fail", he said as he pulled a water container to quench his thirst.

"I do hope you are right and we certainly judged the situation well, this whole thing of being in between and looking over your shoulder all the time is tiring anyway. It is time we either went back home or abandoned this mission and settle here. You all know how we left home and that this unsanctioned mission of ours can go either way in terms of results", Zenzo said with a tired sigh. They remained there as they waited for the great unknown to shed light on itself as to whether they succeeded.

They could have denied knowing anything about this mission and any involvement in it but who knows maybe somebody somewhere knows or saw something that could nail them. They sat at the height of their problems and waited. These were deciding moments for all of them.

Moments that decided whether the decision they took years back was one for life or death. Moments that placed them amongst the most important men in the history of their kingdom or at the bottom of the list where people would rather forget they ever existed.

Life was fair while they lived here. They missed home but were certainly going to miss the cultural life of uMzingwane. They were going to miss the ceremonies they were never again going to participate in. The song and dance that no one else can do except the uMzingwane people.

The ceremonies and rituals, some of which were heart-stopping yet joyous. The warmth of the people, the laughter and the love. They would miss their humour and ubuntu. They were truly a lovely lot of people whom under different circumstances they would have honestly chosen to live amongst.

The arrival of Mahamba was what revived their mission and the need to see it to fruition. Somehow, they were slowly resigning themselves to living amongst these people, besides it was still in the same area as their home. A little distant but still around what they called home.

It is the arrival of the uMzingwane people and their culture that changed things, but the plains remained the same as old. Mahamba came and refused to be assimilated, he reminded them of their people's needs and wants largely of which were imagined but it was what it was so the mission was revived.

Life was such an interesting tale. If you chose a side and genuinely intended to be fruitful on that side it didn't matter whether you had been there before or not, you just naturally made it. On the other hand, if you chose enmity wherever you looked you would see potential enemies and forfeit the joys of peace.

The joys that come with progressive intentions and positive encounters. The joys of new experiences and exposure to other cultures or ways of life. As they sat there in wait realities were beginning to kick in and one hid in his thoughts with little to no hope.

Interesting because they knew the mission happened, and they also believed that it may have happened exactly as planned yet they were resigned to the possibilities of defeat. That sixth sense, the gut feeling that always lays bare what is even as you struggle with trying to convince yourself that it is otherwise.

On the other hand, the king was going through similar yet different feelings. He also felt defeated and wondered if he was worthy of carrying the torch of leadership for his people. He too knew that he did and led well but was beginning to doubt himself. His mind wandered about the ancestors of the land. He wondered if they were involved in all this.

Today's escape had their hand in it for him but why did they allow this to go on for so long with no clues? As he was scratching his head a thought came in, he remembered someone. MADLOMO. She had on several occasions questioned this man and had much to disapprove of him. He began to feel the weight of not listening. What an intelligent woman she was, he marvelled. All the men and people in general in the kingdom could not pick this up yet she did, and no one believed her nor took a minute to ponder about it.

When approached on the issue of Mahamba he believed it was more to do with the fact that he came from where nobody knew. He felt it was only fair to give people the same chances once they were admitted into their space and lived amongst them. He was very sorry; he was enraged, and he felt like a failure. Having failed to detect this for years and at sometimes defended this man yet he was a traitor.

He remembered all the times they went hunting, all the times he was left alone with this man, all the times he sent him on important missions and put men under his care. It was a hard pill to swallow but it was what it was. He had captives in his kingdom, captives that involved his most trusted man. He needed time, time which he didn't have.

After talking to his wife, the prince's father went on back to check on the king who had initially asked to be left alone for a while. He announced his presence and was allowed to come in. They sat down opposite each other and had a deep conversation. For a moment the king came off his chair and sat opposite a man whose life would have been lost today and with whom he could be sitting captive somewhere right now.

It was a scary moment but one which united victims. The two of them were victims and understood what it meant though it did not come to fruition which would be scarier. They had a long heart-to-heart. The king acknowledged that to a greater extent they were far too welcoming.

That a person with an agenda could come and live amongst them for so long was telling of their weakness. They were also too forgiving which came off as naïve to the offenders, but it was who they were. They needed to revise a lot of things, re-do several things and strategize how they were going to go forward.

Having been informed that the other men had escaped the king decided to keep this a top secret while the search for the men went on. When the men who went following their trail returned without success then this matter will be talked about publicly. The ibutho men who had apprehended these men guarded over them.

The prince's father did not return home, but a messenger was sent for MaDlomo that the chief wanted to have a word with her. "MaDlomo, I do not know where to begin on this matter. Whether to begin with thanking you or listening to the tale of how we got here", said the king as he battled calmness. "My king, I understand you and appreciate being in your presence right now", said MaDlomo who had to clear her throat before resuming.

"Ever since I saw and met this man named Mahamba something within me spoke and said there was something amiss about him. I knew something was off about him but could not put a finger on what it was. I engaged several people as you are aware on this issue, but no one seemed willing to listen or to probe further. In the interest of peace and avoiding a case of falsely accusing a man I let it be. Whenever I saw him, it was like I was looking into his spirit, and it was rather a dark place to investigate.

With the recent crowning of our son and the move into the royal grounds, I began to constantly meet with him more than was the case before. This renewed my feelings of suspicion, and I knew I had to do something. One night when I was sleeping, I had a very disturbing vision which I shared with my husband here and we decided to do something about my suspicions.

Since they remained suspicious with no tangible evidence, we decided that for peace's sake and so that we do not falsely accuse a man, we act on it but cautiously. That is when I roped in Mvelo and Thamsanqa here in my service to spy on his movements. They followed him to the mountains sometimes and began to collect the evidence. So that we do not upset you with just suspicion we then engaged Fezela who brought some men from his regiment and put men on the Mahamba's tail.

He began to be convinced more and more that we could be right, and something was fishy with Mahamba's movements. He sometimes met with these men that are now missing and would be together meeting others we hear came from outside through the Imilingo mountains.

Now that it was in the hands of the trusted Fezela we followed his orders while we deliberated on what would happen next but if we all were wrong, we didn't want to upset the kingdom over suspicions, and that is how we ended up where we are today", she said in the closing of her narration.

The king sat there and listened to her narration and each word sunk in. They suspected Mahamba and these men and yet gave them the benefit of the doubt. This meant that it was not only some type of hate they had for them, but this woman's instincts led the way. They exercised all care and caution to not upset anything or anyone while they did the most important work. They protected not only the kingdom but saved his life.

He reflected and sighed. Anyone who did something of this magnitude had to be awarded some type of recognition and so they were going to be awarded the recognition of a sort. He acknowledged everything and personally thanked them. The work was not finished so they waited on what the men who had followed Mahamba's men reported on arrival.

As expected, they brought the men back alive. They were reunited with Mahamba and others and yet there was no time to ask what happened and how the mission failed after such planning. To a degree, they also felt Mahamba's leadership was rushed.

His need to see this through made him overlook certain things and he was impatient. In captivity, they all sat and only their eyes spoke with each other. A long story that was not easy to read whether it was in sorry notes or apologetic tones.

Chiefs were called in from different villages and kingdoms, the leadership came together to deliberate on what to do with these men. In that meeting was a woman who had foiled a key operation. They needed her input, they needed to hear what she had to say. When the meeting was over, they dispersed, and the news of an attempted abduction of the prince and king did rounds for a long time.

The bigger part of that news was how Mahamba had everyone fooled except MaDlomo the warrior queen. A woman with an active sixth sense that picked up things on both the physical and spiritual levels. A woman whose attentiveness saved both the king and prince of uMzingwane. Those who lived with and around Mahamba were terrified. That he could fool a whole kingdom and almost get away with it made them unsure of what else he was capable of.

This was going to make life very difficult for anyone who had come to this place and loved it enough to make it a home. Those who had long lived here and were not ready to go and live anywhere else were terrified as well. This was not going to end well, what if this made them suspects as well? they questioned. It was a tough time for everyone and a tough time for the king of the land.

When the Nkankezi kingdom was contacted over this attempt their king said they should face the music because their actions had cost the two kingdoms a lot. He said their attempts were not of peace, unity or progress yet the two kingdoms had long agreed on peaceful and progressive existence alongside each other. He humbly asked the king and people of uMzingwane to forgive them for their actions on their own and to continue observing peace, and progressive existence amongst other positive things.

They were punished and served sentences in the kingdom under heavy guard. Some of them fell ill and died while others eventually returned to their kingdom. They returned in shame and were received in shame. Legend had it that they did not live long even after their return home.

Mahamba was always homesick, he had always hoped and wished on the day of his return which he planned to be heroic, he believed his people would applaud and cheer, that his people would love and chant his name, but it didn't happen. His people were ashamed to claim him while others believed he had long died while he lived in uMzingwane.

Things normalised, life resumed and after some time the king fell ill. His health continued to deteriorate and one day he called for a meeting with his chiefs and council of elders. In that meeting, he told them that his health was deteriorating, and he was unsure if he will recover his full health back. They talked about many issues around the kingdom and eventualities to which he nominated the mother of the prince to become regent queen. She was more than capable and well, they all will be in safe hands.

It was deliberated for a good long while until everyone agreed that she should be called in and informed. Thandiwe Dlomo had become regent queen on the premise that she was the queen mother who would hold the position until her son was old enough to lead. She was also a warrior, one that had led them into triumph where no one else knew they were in danger. She sensed things, she saw things and she was on top of things. Other than that, she led well with due diligence.

A ceremony was held, one to officially install her as the regent queen. She was blessed. She was praised. She was honoured and it was a good day. One that the kingdom desperately needed after recent events. It was uplifting and it was a breath of fresh air to see the people merry once more, united, and hopeful together.

When the ceremony was concluded, it rained splashes of hope. She led them heroically through wars and triumphed. She was brave, she was of a sound mind, and she was spiritually connected. The king recovered and lived for a good long while but refused to be involved in the leadership of the kingdom. When they needed his counsel, he offered it. He spent a good part of his time with the prince. He did not go hunting nor did he do any activity that exerted his body, though he recovered he was still weak and chose to stay away from pressure.

On his passing, there was great sorrow in the kingdom. All the procedures and days to be observed before his burial was filled with sadness. He was laid to rest eventually, and the mood remained sombre all around. He was going to be remembered. A king for his people. A king with a heart and yet his story will always carry the weight of Mahamba's saga.

Nsikayezwe grew to take the ropes of power from his mother. A fearless queen whose bosom gave life repeatedly to the kingdom of uMzingwane. A fearless woman who held the knife on its sharp edge when the need arose. He learnt a lot from the king and took lessons from many encounters in his life.

His childhood stories began to make sense as well. He rose to the helm of power under the care and counsel of his father. Both his parents were there and key on his journey. Just like his father he was very calm and calculated. Just like his great grandmother who visited him in the cave in the mountains alongside another and then his great granddad he was not quick to speak.

He spoke like he counted his words and sized their effects before he uttered them. Just like the previous king he had the utmost love and care for the people. Just like many before him, he was an example of ubuntu. Things had taken a twist and turn during and after the Mahamba saga. Some changes had become permanent, maybe just maybe the future would bring along its own stories and change once more happens after all it is the only constant.

# Epilogue

Hoping you had a safe journey with the people of uMzingwane kingdom to and from the mountains.
Ubuntu mabande!